Katie,

This book symbolizes that dreams can come true. I love your music and your art. Please never give it up, because your art matters. May you find inspiration in what you decide to do.

Kevin Moose

Swear An Oath

Swear An Oath

Kevin Morse

Copyright © 2010 by Kevin Morse.

Library of Congress Control Number: 2010909951
ISBN: Hardcover 978-1-4535-3526-4
Softcover 978-1-4535-3525-7
E-book 978-1-4535-3527-1

All rights reserved. No part of this book may be reproduced or transmitted in any form or by any means, electronic or mechanical, including photocopying, recording, or by any information storage and retrieval system, without permission in writing from the copyright owner.

This is a work of fiction. Names, characters, places and incidents either are the product of the author's imagination or are used fictitiously, and any resemblance to any actual persons, living or dead, events, or locales is entirely coincidental.

This book was printed in the United States of America.

To order additional copies of this book, contact:
Xlibris Corporation
1-888-795-4274
www.Xlibris.com
Orders@Xlibris.com
83184

CHAPTER 1

"What have we got, Patriots? A monarchy or a republic?" addressed the chairman of the meeting he was presiding over. The men at this meeting were all older men wearing white wigs and colonial clothing. The scene looked like a basic town hall meeting in a small New England town with its history being preserved in the community.

"A REPUBLIC!" the Patriots yelled in loud exclamation.

"Ah! A republic if you can keep it. Right now we are losing it. The Constitution and Bill of Rights are eroding away like sands in an hourglass. We are looking at a tyrannical state unless we inform the masses. Most of the police are running around on steroids. They have no idea the animals they are becoming. When we were in the force, we had a code of conduct we lived by. Where is it today? How far gone has the nation turned? Patriots, an emergency call to action is needed in these times. We are in desperate times, and desperate times call for desperate measures. We need to find a new member to lead us in this fight. Someone who has the knowledge on what this country stands for and the grit it takes to save this republic. So, Patriots, give me some ideas."

One of the Patriots spoke up. "Why don't we get somebody from the Michigan militia? They are certainly qualified."

Another one responded, "Now, I would agree, but remember the Hutaree militia was set up by the FBI. You have to be very careful when you're looking at the militias. There is always somebody trying to infiltrate those groups."

"Okay, how about a Tea Party supporter?"

"Again, if they would have stayed grassroots, maybe, but they let themselves be hijacked with politicians. A politician is the last kind of person we need."

Then a huge wave of voices started to yell and scream all at once. A mass hysteria was coming over the group when the chairmen bellowed, "PATRIOTS."

"Enough of this! This isn't getting us anywhere. The usual suspects aren't the answer right now. What we need is a diamond in the rough. Someone who is well under anybody's radar and someone who has pretty much gone unnoticed from everybody in the course of their life. Now, Patriots, quick bickering and find me this individual right now!"

10:14 a.m.

Alan Williams is a private investigator, but these days Alan was usually unemployed. Work was hard to come by in his hometown of Jackson, Michigan. Michigan was in a statewide economic depression. The city of Jackson had always seen its share of hard times since factory shops started being outsourced in the 1980s. Alan was in a constant state of agitation. Alan was not happy unless he was working. Fortunately, Melissa Henneman was there to keep him company.

Melissa, standing five feet ten inches tall with her jet-black hair, silky smooth and flowing past her shoulders, did her best to keep Alan sane and in control. Melissa took on the role of being Alan's assistant and girlfriend for a year now. Melissa always felt sorry for Alan for his extreme introverted personality that kept him inside his office researching forensics, esoteric mysteries, and the occult. Melissa stayed with Alan in his office to help assist with clients, but she felt compelled to pry Alan away from the computer so Alan would maintain somewhat of a social life and a healthy relationship between them.

Alan, as a kid, followed Sherlock Holmes; and his favorite show was the *X-Files*. Melissa met Alan at a karaoke bar. Alan's photographic memory impressed Melissa when Alan would sing in front of the crowd. Melissa particularly liked it when Alan sang "East Bound and Down" by Jerry Reed. It is the theme song to Melissa's favorite movie, the classic Burt Reynolds film, *Smokey and the Bandit*.

Alan got a bachelor's degree in criminal justice and was on top of his class. Alan's eccentric personality and beliefs kept him from landing a job in the police force. The police could not handle Alan's lone wolf mentality. They did not view him as being a team player. The police saw Alan as someone who would eventually become a liability and an embarrassment for them. Another issue with Alan was the fact that he was a strict constitutionalist.

Alan did everything by the book. Alan took very seriously the civil rights of citizens and criminals. He would take issue when the police would try to conduct searches without a warrant and without probable cause. Alan had the Bill of Rights memorized and would constantly cite the Fourth Amendment in front of others. The police were not worried about the rules per se, they were more concerned with getting results. Some in the police were caught breaking the rules. They were nonchalant in their demeanor, and their attitude was letting the chips fall where they may. Alan saw too much willing on the part of the police to risk suppressed evidence. Alan went out of his way to make sure the rules were followed. The police department hated Alan for this, and it left Alan to work in the private sector as a PI.

Alan Williams was sitting behind the desk of his office one sunny Monday morning when his telephone rang at ten fourteen in the morning. "Hello, Alan Williams here."

"Alan, Mark Lewis. You remember me?"

"Oh, yeah! You went to school with me in college."

"Yeah, well, I am need of your help. Could you come to Detroit and meet with me?"

"Right now?"

"Yes, right now. Can you make it by 2:00 p.m.?"

"Yes, 2:00 p.m. is fine."

"All right, meet me in the Ramada Inn, just north of Metro Airport, suite 133."

"Okay, I'll be there."

"Sounds like the commencement of a case," said Melissa.

Alan was puzzled by the phone call. Alan could not help feeling uneasy that an old classmate calls out of the blue and asks for his help. At the same time, Alan likes to sink his teeth into some intrigue, and this had the earmarks of a mystery.

"Who's driving?" asked Melissa. Melissa hoped Alan would let her drive.

"You can drive this time," said Alan.

Alan grabbed his brown leather jacket and brown fedora hat off the rack and put it on his five-feet-eight-inch skinny frame. The hat is a replica of Indiana Jones'. His father gave it to him as a Christmas present. Alan has worn the hat ever since that Christmas Day. Alan gave the keys to Melissa as they took off in Alan's 1977 black Pontiac Firebird. The classic car had always been beloved by Alan and Melissa, especially after seeing the movie *Smokey and the Bandit*.

Driving on Interstate 94, Alan put in a Def Leppard CD. Def Leppard is Alan's favorite music band. Alan, while he was in college, saw Def Leppard in concert. It is one of the very few Alan has ever attended. He instantly became impressed with the combination of expression and technique they put in their rock music. "Pour Some Sugar on Me" started playing as Melissa asked who they were meeting. Melissa was one who just liked to talk to Alan while he was on a case. The way in which Alan's brain worked fascinated Melissa. Melissa did not pretend to be an expert in criminal investigation; she just liked being there supporting Alan. Alan appreciated Melissa for it for he knew he'd be lonely without her.

"We are meeting a former classmate of mine from college, Mark Lewis. Mark and I were both into WWE Wrestling and saw some shows together." Melissa then interrupted by saying, "Wait, you watched WWE wrestling?"

"Yes."

"You actually had a life before you were turned into the monster that you are now!" Alan always chuckled at Melissa's humor.

"As a matter of fact, I did. I recall having a blast. Mark was usually my tag team partner in our mock investigations in school. We got to be friends while going to school. We were both fans of the Heartbreak Kid, and he turned out to be the hero in the show that we watched."

"Wow!" interjected Melissa. "Each day you amaze me. Is there anything else I do not know about you? So what do you think he wants now?"

"Watch out, Melissa. Highway patrol is behind that bridge." Melissa was very careful not to speed, but the constant presence of law enforcement reminded Alan of the evidence of the rising police state that was happening inside the United States. Among the variety of topics that Alan researches, Alan had fears that the United States is becoming a high-tech police state. Alan concluded that there was a Big Brother surveillance system watching the citizenry, just like in the George Orwell novel *1984*.

"I have no idea. I haven't seen him since he transferred to a different campus, which was about three years ago. I do not know what happened to him since."

The mood certainly changed at 1:45 p.m. when Alan and Melissa arrived at the Ramada Inn. The entire hotel was littered with police cars, flashing lights (which Alan referred to as disco lights), and ambulances.

"Melissa, it is attempted murder, at the very least!" cried Alan.

"You mean your friend?"

"I don't believe it was a coincidence that we were summoned to come here and we find all these disco lights without there being a connection."

As soon as Melissa could park the car, Alan rushed out the door and raced inside the hotel. Alan would only get as far as the lobby where many policemen were hovering around blocking a path to the elevator. Then the receptionist saw Alan looking around and asked, "Sir, may I help you?"

"Yes, suite 133, please," asked Alan in his typical charming voice. Alan was a perfect gentleman when he spoke in public.

"Oh, I am so sorry, sir. There's been a . . . a suicide." The receptionist tried to talk as she was stumbling over her own words.

"Suicide!" exclaimed Alan as his voice just raised in disbelief and anger, far different than his usual suave voice. Hearing the word "suicide" agitated Alan because he knew if Mark was the dead body in suite 133, he would not have called asking him to meet him and then commit suicide. Alan started to scream almost, "I want to see who is in charge here!"

The receptionist, starting to panic, tried to calm Alan down. "Sir, perhaps you should leave and come back later when the police are done."

That just got Alan angrier. "No, I want to see the person in charge now!"

At this point, the police overheard what was going on at the reception desk, and they started making their way over. Melissa, not liking the look of the men and always having Alan's back, said to him, "Maybe it would be better if we come back later. Let's go, Alan."

"Melissa, I am not leaving here until I talk to the person in charge."

Then a loud female voice echoed from across the lobby, "Well, you got her." Immediately, Alan knew who it was.

"Detective Sara Lorenzo," Alan said in a sarcastic manner. Detective Sara Lorenzo stood just shy of six feet, strawberry blond hair, a slim, curvaceous figure, and rosy cheeks.

"And Alan Williams. Still believing in conspiracy theories? It's all right, boys, I'll handle this. Who is your girlfriend?"

"Melissa Henneman."

"Well, I never thought anyone would hang out with you, Alan, but all props to you, Melissa, for having the guts."

Alan was getting impatient with Lorenzo. "Can we stop with the put-downs?"

"Yes, Alan. Let's get down to business. What do you want to see me for, and what are doing here?"

"I got a phone call from Mark Lewis at 10:14 a.m. saying to meet him at 2:00 p.m. He told me to meet him here."

"What did he want to meet you about?"

"He didn't say."

"Well, we will never know because he committed suicide today."

Melissa gave a look of horror upon hearing the detective.

"Suicide. That is a pretty quick conclusion. What makes you think so?" said Alan with confidence, knowing that Lorenzo was wrong.

"We found him hung on the ceiling hook with a rope, and there is a note."

"May I see the note?"

Detective Lorenzo held the note in the evidence bag for Alan to see.

Alan became irritated when he saw that the note had been typed.

"This note has been typed, this is not a suicide!"

Detective Lorenzo, sort of expecting this from Alan, amused the crowd by saying, "Oh, here we go now, another one of your conspiracy theories. Boys, let me introduce you to Alan Williams, the conspiracy theorist. If you got a crime, he's got a conspiracy theory for it. Just a second, let me get your tin foil hat for you."

"No, I already got a hat, thank you, and it is not a conspiracy theory. No one wanting to commit suicide would type their suicide note, and besides, why would Mark ask me to see him and then commit suicide later? That makes no sense."

"Maybe he was already thinking about it and wanted your advice before doing the deed and decided not to wait any longer."

Alan, who could not believe what he was hearing, interjected, "That's ludicrous! If that was the case, why wouldn't he call a family member or someone close by? Why would he call me for that?"

"I don't know, but stay in town. I am going to want to talk to you before we are done. Did you know Mr. Lewis?"

"I knew him but had not seen him in three years. May I see the body?" inquired Alan.

Detective Lorenzo, reluctant to let Alan anywhere near a crime scene, decided to go ahead. "Yeah, okay, Alan. We need someone to identify the body if you can do it for us."

Detective Lorenzo took Alan and Melissa up to suite 133 to show the body of Mark Lewis. Mark's room was open, and it was as Detective Lorenzo described. Mark's body was hanging on a ceiling hook in the middle of the room by a rope. The bed had been slightly moved from its original position.

Lorenzo asked, "Is that Mark Lewis?"

"Yeah, that's how I remember him, except for the glasses. He didn't wear glasses when he was in college."

"All right then, coroner, you may remove the body."

"Who discovered the body?" asked Alan.

"The housekeeper making her daily rounds came in at about 1:00 p.m."

"Is there anything else, Detective?"

"It can wait till we get to my office."

"Then let's go."

As Alan had one last look at Mark's body, he saw the glasses again. The only object that was odd in the crime scene, and then Alan shouted about the glasses.

"What's that?" asked Lorenzo.

"He is wearing glasses."

"Wow, is it any wonder you did not make detective?"

Alan, starting to get frustrated, said, "You found him wearing glasses on his body, didn't you?"

"Yeah, so what?"

In a loud voice, Alan shouted, "No one commits suicide with their glasses on!"

"Boy, you and your conspiracy theories never stop."

Alan, frustrated even more, continued, "Someone with glasses, if they were going to do the deed, would take their glasses off just like they would if they were going to bed." Alan was feeling like the teacher when all his students are struggling with a particular lesson and the teacher has run out of tricks to use.

Lorenzo was looking at Alan like he was crazy. "Look, Alan, we are professionals. We know what we are doing here. This is a suicide if I ever saw one. Now let's get out of here discuss this further down at the station."

"Would you mind if Melissa and I follow you in my car?"

"No, that would be fine."

CHAPTER 2

Making their way out of the hotel and into the black Firebird Trans Am, Melissa asked Alan, "What is up with you two? You two seem to have some sort of history together."

"Sara Lorenzo was one of my teachers in college. She was my least favorite teacher because she was the only one not to give a 4.0 grade in her class. I think she is totally misguided in the ways of this profession. Half the time she did not show up herself, then the half she was there, she was completely wrong in her philosophy in policing. She would argue that if the prosecution wanted a bench trial, they ought to have that right over the right of the defendant to a trial by jury. That is totally against the Sixth and Seventh Amendments. She is a strong supporter of the Patriot Act signed by President Bush in 2001. She believes that reasonable suspicion is all you need to conduct a search. She believes that the police have the right to perform 'sneak and peeks' and that the searches are constitutionally protected. Of course, we know they are not. That is totally against the Fourth Amendment. Basically, she thinks America is a police state and not a republic and the police can do whatever the hell they want. I complained about her professionalism to the assistant dean, and she agreed to have her reevaluated as a full-time faculty instructor. Anyway, I wrote my thesis on how the government is intentionally eroding away our civil liberties, and she has had me labeled as a conspiracy theorist since college. Man, we have got to get back to the Constitution."

"Amen, brother. Preach on," shouted Melissa. Melissa could tell when Alan talked about the Constitution; Alan's eyes would light up. This excited Melissa. Alan could effectively communicate with Melissa the problems with the country as Alan saw it. Somehow this made sense with Melissa. As complex and elaborate as the subject matter was, not only did it remind

Melissa that Alan was intelligent, but it also proved that she could trust him with her life. For that, Melissa felt safe around Alan.

"Maybe I should have been a preacher instead of a private investigator?"

"No, Alan, what you are doing is so needed right now in order to turn this country around. Never doubt that for a second."

"Thanks, Melissa."

"You're welcome. What do you think Detective Lorenzo wants to see us about?" Melissa's voice oozed with sarcasm at the detective's name.

"She probably wants to give us the third degree. Get us on a terrorism charge. Something along those lines."

"Why bother going then? Let's just make a run for it?"

"No, Melissa. Let me handle the talking. If they start getting in your face, ask for a lawyer. Use your Fifth Amendment right. Cite them *Miranda v. Arizona*. It is still a constitutional republic, last time I checked."

"Okay, Alan, you always seem to know best."

"You know what gets me the most though, Melissa?"

"What's that?"

"Police officers, politicians, and military, all of them, swear an oath to protect and defend the Constitution. Instead, what has happened, it has been dragged through the sewer. Does anyone take their oath seriously or understand what it means anymore?"

CHAPTER 3

It was about 3:21 p.m., when Melissa and Alan arrived at the police station. They followed Detective Lorenzo to her office.

"Okay, you two have seat right there," ordered Lorenzo. "The first thing is, I do not believe you're telling the whole truth about the real reason why you came to see Mark Lewis."

Alan responded, "Did I do something with my eyes that made me give it away or are your interviewing technique skills as sharp as they once were?"

Lorenzo pounded her fist down on her desk. "Damn it, Alan! We are not in class anymore. You're lucky I still happen to think Lewis's death is still a suicide or I'd have you arrested for suspicion of murder."

Alan somewhat puzzled asked, "I am a bit confused then. Are you going to charge us or not?"

"No, I am not charging you."

"Well, can we go?"

"No, because that is not the reason why you're here."

Alan and Melissa looked at each other more confused than ever. "Why are we here then?"

Detective Lorenzo began to show photographs of a definitive murder. "There was a murder yesterday over by the Joe Louis Arena. We found the victim's body like this. I am going to bring in Lieutenant Chris Patrick to fill you in on the rest of the details."

As Lorenzo went to get her supervisor, Chris Patrick, Alan, and Melissa were left looking at some very disturbing pictures of a white middle-aged man, lying on the ground. His throat has been slit wide open and his tongue was hanging out, but not where you normally expect to find a tongue. Then a middle-aged African-American man who was a bit on the bulky side walked into the room.

"Alan Williams, Lieutenant Chris Patrick, homicide. I have heard so much about you from Detective Lorenzo."

"All of it bad, I hope," mocked Alan.

Lieutenant Patrick laughed with amusement as if he had known the whole story.

"Listen, Alan. I think you're an eccentric fellow, but you could be of a valuable asset to this case." commented Patrick. "From what I have learned from Lorenzo, you have some sort of expertise in the occult."

"That's correct," said Alan interested in where Patrick was going with this.

"Well, we think this is the work of the occult and would value your opinion on this one."

"What do you want me to do exactly?"

"I want you to assist us on this case."

"What? Really?"

"Yes, seriously, Alan. See, this is case is too big and too important not to pull all the resources that are available to us. We really have no one that has a knack for the occult in this department. That is why we want you to help us."

"I would be happy to help in any way that I can," Alan said in his suave, gentlemanly voice. "What is the victim's name?" Alan's voice sounded smooth and deep. His vocabulary and demeanor was old-fashioned like he came out of the 1930s. Alan was like a British gentleman with an American accent.

"The victim's name is Casey Thomas. He is a banker out in Novi. Now, we think this is the work of a satanic cult. Would you agree, Mr. Williams?"

"Yes, I would agree, but satanic could mean different things to different people. Give me a few hours and I think I can work out the group behind this."

"He was found on the shore of the Detroit River yesterday. It appears as if he was washed up on shore, as far as we can tell. He died from the laceration you see on his throat. His tongue had been cut off and now you see it hanging out from this throat. Why cut the tongue?"

"Well, it could be some sort of symbolism that this person ran his mouth off too much or it could be a signature left by the killer. Have you seen any other victims with their tongue hanging out?"

"No."

Just then, a man with a manila folder interrupted, "Sir, toxicology just came back."

"Thank you, bring it here," said Lieutenant Patrick. As Patrick was going over the toxicology report, he seemed quite puzzled. "This is interesting."

"What's that?" inquired Alan.

"The victim's body was doped up with formaldehyde, thimerosal, caustic soda, hydrochloric acid, sheep's blood, and charcoal, and the list goes on and on."

"How did that get inside him?"

"I don't know, but if Casey Thomas wouldn't have had his throat slit, this shit might have killed him eventually anyway." Patrick paused for a moment and then refocused his attention back on Alan. "So, Mr. Williams, will you help us?"

Alan would have preferred to work on his friend's murder, but he couldn't refuse the opportunity to turn down a job. Alan needed the work bad. "Yes, I will help you on the Thomas murder, but what about the Mark Lewis murder?

"Murder! Lorenzo, I thought you said it was suicide?"

Lorenzo, a bit irritated with Alan's insinuation, "It is a suicide, and Mr. Williams here seems to think otherwise."

"I see, well, Mr. Williams, you don't worry about that one. We are calling it a suicide and we just want your help with the murder. Now you can investigate as if you are in charge of the case because for now you are. When you have got something, report immediately to Detective Lorenzo. Are we clear on that?"

"Yes, quite clear." Alan said reluctantly, but enough to make Lorenzo and Patrick assured he knew the rules.

"Very good. If anything changes, I will call you."

CHAPTER 4

Melissa and Alan got back into their Trans Am. Just stepping outside of the police station was like a breath of fresh air to them. "Well," said Melissa, "what are you going to do, Alan?"

"I'll tell you what we are going to do. We are going to solve both of these murders."

"Even though the lieutenant said to stay away from it."

"The hell with that! They can't scare me. Mark Lewis was my friend, and I will be damned if I am going to let his murder go unsolved and let it be ruled a suicide, if I can't do everything in my power to do something about it."

"All right, where do you want to start? There is not much to go on."

"We'll start with his fiancée."

"Fiancée?"

"Well, she was his fiancée when we went to college. I do not know if they ever married. I need to know about his life from the last three years. Since Mark can't tell us, maybe his fiancée can."

"Okay, who is she?"

"That's the problem, I never met her. I only know her first name, Kayla."

"Well, that does not help much."

"Now hold on, Melissa. I still have her e-mail address."

"How do you have her e-mail address?"

"Mark and I were working on this Weapons of Mass Destruction scenario assignment in college. Well, one day he forgot his assignment at home. It was only saved on his hard drive at home. He needed a way to send it to school. So I suggested to Mark to have his fiancée e-mail to me on my user-based account, which Mark didn't have at the time. Since I never delete my e-mails, it should still be saved."

"You still remember things like that? You are incredible and amazing."

"I am what I am. So I will e-mail Kayla and ask to meet her for an interview. But first, let's find the nearest library. There is something about the photographs that Lieutenant Patrick showed us that I want to check out."

CHAPTER 5

Meanwhile, Detective Lorenzo went to meet with the pathologist, Dr. Ordonez, about his report on the Lewis death. Lorenzo expected this report to be quick and without any surprises. Lorenzo walks in the morgue and greets the doctor.

"Let me guess, doctor. Suicide, death as a result of strangulation."

Dr. Ordonez, already knowing Lorenzo for her cockiness, fired back at her. "Wrong, Lorenzo! Wrong on both counts, back to school for you, Lorenzo!

"What!" exclaimed Lorenzo as if the good doctor was just pulling her leg.

"Come here and have a closer look."

Lorenzo crept up to the body, having no clue what the pathologist was about to show her.

The pathologist turned the back of the victim's head and pointed out that there was blunt-force trauma on the back of Lewis's head. "The blunt-force trauma was what killed this man. The trauma to the back of the head happened before the victim was hanged."

"So, doctor, let me get this straight. You're saying that this was a murder intended to look like suicide?"

"Unless you know a way in which a dead man can hang himself, yes, that is exactly what I am saying. The rope marks on the neck are also inconsistent with neck marks of a live hanging. The impressions are not as distinct and deep."

"Do you know the time of death, doctor?"

"Between noon and twelve thirty."

"Hmmm . . . Well, so far Williams's story checks out."

"What do you mean?"

"Williams received a phone call from the victim at 10:14 a.m. on the day of the murder. Damn, I can't believe I am saying that. Anything else you can tell me, doctor?"

"Not until toxicology comes back."

"All right then, thanks, doctor."

"Say, how was your date with Emily last night?"

"I think it went great. I took her to Margarita's Mexican Restaurant. Then we went and saw the new *Star Trek* movie."

"Was it good? Everyone around here says it is."

"Oh, yes. Emily and I both enjoyed it. I thought it was the best *Star Trek* movie."

"What did you think of Emily?"

"Oh, she is beautiful, intelligent, and just flat out pleasant. She has a healthy and positive attitude toward life."

"Well, I really wish you well with her. Sometimes, I think you spend too much time down here in the morgue, but that's just my opinion."

CHAPTER 6

4:43 p.m.

Melissa and Alan walked into the closest public library they could find in Detroit. Alan went to the help desk and asked the clerk, "Where would I find all the books you have on Freemasonry?"

Melissa was stunned by the question, "Freemasons?"

"Freemasons have always had a long and controversial history in this country. They have been involved in some of the most brutal murders ever in the United States. Most notably, the murder of Captain Morgan"

"Captain Morgan? You mean the guy on the Puerto Rican rum? Man, I would love to get wasted on that tonight."

"No, Melissa. The rum is named after Sir Henry Morgan, Caribbean privateer from seventeenth-century Wales."

"What, you don't have a 'little captain in you'?" said Melissa sarcastically.

"No, I'm talking about Captain William Morgan, Freemason in the nineteenth century."

"Oh, that Captain Morgan," said Melissa with sheer amazement at Alan's incredible knowledge. First, Melissa was impressed that Alan knew who the rum was named for when she didn't. Second, Melissa was impressed with the way Alan could explain about people from history that nobody she knew could.

"In 1826, Captain Morgan, who fought in the War of 1812, at least that is what his tombstone says, published an expose on Freemasonry, the Blue Lodges, and the three degrees. The Freemasons did not like what Captain Morgan did, because they wanted their order to remain a secret in the United States. The Freemasons abducted him, read him the riot act, and then voted to kill him. Essentially, he was murdered."

"Didn't anything happen to those Freemasons for killing Captain Morgan"

"No, nothing ever happened with the murder of Captain William Morgan."

"How come?"

"The answer to that is going to sound like a conspiracy, but that is what it exactly is, a conspiracy."

"Explain."

"In 1869, an ex-Mason who lived during the time of the Morgan murder, by the name of Charles G. Finney, wrote *The Character, Claims, and Practical Workings of Freemasonry*. In it, Finney said that there could never be any justice for Captain Morgan. Morgan was from Batavia, New York. You take the sheriff, judge, and the jury that was in Batavia or any American town during that time and chances are they would all be Freemasons. Freemasonry was growing and expanding in the United States and, as claimed by Finney, worked themselves in important positions in government. Do you think a Freemason jury would convict one of their own, especially in light of the circumstances?"

"I see your point, but how is all this still known then?"

"It is written on Morgan's tombstone, which is still in Batavia. I am sure the library has it here, I can show it to you."

Just then, Alan turned to the librarian and asked him to also get a book on Captain Morgan's tombstone.

Melissa, still somewhat puzzled on the Freemason angle, said to Alan, "My grandfather is the sweetest old man I ever knew, and he was a Freemason. I just can't imagine my grandfather would be involved in something like that."

"Most likely not, and I also had a grandfather who was a Freemason, and I know my grandfather would have nothing to do with brutal men like that. You have to understand something, though most Freemasons only go through the first three degrees. They are referred to as the blue degrees. I like to refer to them as porch masons. There are actually thirty-three degrees of Freemasonry. The porch masons have no idea what they are in for when they are initiated into the secret society. An initiate is blindfolded during the first-degree rite upon walking into the Masonic chamber. It symbolizes the initiate as a fool, because the hierarchy of the order are laughing at him and mocking him in secret for they are not telling the true nature of the order. He may not even know there are thirty other degrees after the third degree. This ritual form has been replicated in other secret societies."

"Well, what are Freemasons really about?"

"All right, in the blue degrees, the first three degrees, the Freemasons are told that they are looking for the lost name of God. This is why it is required that you must believe in a god for you to become a Freemason. They never learn it in the blue degrees. The lost name of God is not revealed to them until the thirteenth degree. The name is not really lost. However, it is just the sacred name of the Mason's god. The sacred name of God is composed of three identities of God. The three identities of God are Yahweh, the name of the Jewish God, shortened to Yah. Second is Baal. Baal is a demon in Christianity. Some Christian writings even have Baal as Satan itself. Third is Osiris, the sun god of ancient Egypt, which is shortened to just On. Now take the three syllables which the masons claim are their three identities of God, Yah-Baal-On, what do you have?"

"Ya . . . Bal . . . On?" mumbled Melissa, trying to sound it out.

"Jahbuhlun."

"Jah . . . buhl . . . un . . . yeah, what is that?"

"Jahbuhlun, not Jesus, is the name of the Freemason's god. In fact, three masons will grip each others' hands and chant, 'Jahbuhlun, Jahbuhlun, Jahbuhlun, Jehovah,' during the lost-name rite."

"Sir, I hate to interrupt you, but you can find your information upstairs in section HS 403," the librarian interrupted. Alan thanked the librarian.

Alan continued, "Now where was I? Oh yeah, Jahbuhlun. If you asked a grand master of Freemason about the rite, he may or may not confirm it for you. What they will always deny, however, is that Jahbuhlun is another word for Satan."

"Satan! Freemasons is a satanic cult!"

"Yes."

"Why, that's incredible."

"It is, and remember when I told the lieutenant that satanic could mean different things to different people. Freemasons have been good at covering the truth about their secret society for hundreds of years. So good they have kept the secret from their own porch masons."

"This is fascinating, but what does this have to do with our murder?"

"The way in which Casey Thomas died, his throat was slit wide-open and tongue cut off, I am trying to remember, but something tells me there is a Freemason connection. I am here looking through these books searching for the answer. Before I look for the answer, here is Captain Morgan's tombstone."

The picture showed a large monument statue with an inscription written on the front. The statue was silver in color and made of granite. The inscription said the following:

> Sacred to the memory of Wm Morgan,
> a native of Virginia.
> A Capt. in the War of 1812.
> A respectable citizen of Batavia
> and a martyr to the freedom of
> writing, printing, and speaking the
> truth. He was abducted from near
> this spot in the year 1826, by Freemasons
> and murdered for revealing the secrets
> of their Order.

The inscription went on to say that the truth about what was written of Morgan's tombstone could be found in the court records of Genesee County.

Melissa felt bored the next ten minutes, and it felt more like twenty. The atmosphere of the library was dull, and she was getting ready to go to sleep. She knew, however, that Alan was on to something and what he was doing was extremely important and valuable to the investigation. She did not want to talk to Alan while he was researching and make him lose focus and concentration. She knew Alan long enough that when he is committed to something, he follows through with it every time.

Then she thought about what Alan said about the Freemasons being a satanic cult and her grandfather. She felt sorry that her grandfather could be duped and fooled into such a hideous organization as she started to remember her childhood days with him. She remembered how her grandfather would make her laugh when she was a little girl. She still missed her grandfather after losing him to cancer on a Christmas Eve six years ago. A most solemn Christmas it was that year. She started to miss him a little more today after hearing Alan's account of Freemasonry and hoped justice may come for Sean Thomas and Mark Lewis, when it did not come for Captain William Morgan almost two hundred years ago. Melissa was practically daydreaming when she was awoken by Alan's exclamation.

"I got it!" Alan said with a bit of glee. "Look at this, Melissa."

"What do you have, Alan?"

"I knew there was a Freemason connection. You remembered I said that an initiate is blindfolded in the first-degree rite as symbolism of the hierarchy mocking and laughing at the fool. Each degree has a ritual and an oath that the initiate has to swear to. Well, in the first-degree oath, it says, 'Binding myself under no less penalty than that of having my throat cut across, my tongue torn out by its roots, and my body buried in the rough sands of the sea, at low-water mark, where the tide ebbs and flows in twenty-four hours, should I ever knowingly violate this my Entered Apprentice obligation.' You see here, Melissa. Casey Thomas must have been a first-degree mason and he violated his oath. Our killer is a Freemason."

"Oh my God! This oath describes what we saw in those photographs!"

"Yes."

"Wait . . . are you saying that every Freemason has to take this oath?"

"Yes."

"Then my grandfather also took this oath."

"Mine too."

Melissa's face turned somber and looked like she was about to cry.

Alan went to console Melissa. He told her not to cry and that they should channel their grief and pain into finding Casey's and Mark's killers. Melissa nodded her head.

"Okay, Melissa. Keep your chin up. Don't let the enemy see that you're weak. Someone else might be in need of us, who may also be grieving. Let's go e-mail Mark's girl, Kayla, and find her."

With that, Alan borrowed one of the library's computers and sent an e-mail to Kayla. After Melissa and Alan left the library, they drove back home to Jackson and called it a night. There was nothing more they could do that night and hoped they would get an e-mail response when they returned home.

CHAPTER 7

Detective Lorenzo was beside herself in awe. She was so sure the Lewis's homicide was a suicide. Even more astonishing was the fact that Alan Williams had nailed it right from the beginning. She went to Patrick's office to report this extraordinary change of events.

"Sir, do you have time to see me?"

"Yes, Lorenzo. Whaddya got for me?"

"I just spoke with Dr. Ordonez downstairs in the morgue and he just ruled the Lewis suicide a murder."

"Well, that was what Alan Williams was saying. Why did he think it was a murder and why did you think it was suicide?"

"Sir, I thought it could not have been plainer. It looked like your garden-variety suicide. He hung from the ceiling in the middle of the hotel room. He had a suicide note. There were no apparent indications of foul play."

"Why did Williams suspect murder?"

"I thought he was just going off on a tantrum or something. He mentioned he was phoned by Lewis in the morning to meet with him there. He saw the note and claimed it was a fake."

"How did he know it was a fake?"

"Because it had been typed."

"Go on," Patrick seemed more intrigued.

"That's it. Oh, wait . . . yes, he mentioned something about the glasses."

"What about them?"

"Lewis was wearing them and he shouldn't have been."

"You know, I would not have bet on it, I am trying to remember, but I can't say that I have ever seen a suicide with glasses or a typed note. What a fascinating brain on that guy. What was the cause of death?"

"Dr. Ordonez said it was blunt-force trauma to the back of the head. Man, wait till Williams hears about this. He is going to give me the ultimate I-told-you-so speech. Ironically, in college, he would always tell me it was a capital mistake to theorize before data. I guess he was right there. So, Lieutenant, how do you want me to handle this? We've got two murders on our plate now!"

"Lorenzo, you stay on the Lewis case."

"What about Williams?"

"Nothing changes with him. It's good we have his help on the Thomas murder now. He just became more valuable to us."

"You don't want me to tell him about Lewis?"

"No, he does not need to know right now. Let's maximize our resources and not get sidetracked."

"All right, sir. I will go down and get Lewis's personal effects and try to dig up a lead."

CHAPTER 8

Melissa and Alan were certainly glad to be in their home office after a long and eventful day. They wanted to get some sleep because they had a feeling it was going to be a long day tomorrow. Alan immediately turned his computer to check his e-mail. While Alan was waiting for the computer to boot, a question popped into Melissa's head.

"What if this Kayla chick does not respond to you? What if she is already dead herself? What would the next course of action be?"

"Good question, Melissa."

"Why thank you, Alan."

"Honestly, I had not anticipated that possibility. I am not sure yet." I guess we would have to go to Lorenzo and give her what we got."

"That sucks! I can't stand the way she talks down to you. Besides, everything else you have told me about her."

Alan opened his inbox and found there was one new message.

"I got an e-mail Melissa, and it's from . . . Kayla Gagne! Looks like Lorenzo's going to have to wait a bit longer."

"All right, what does it say?" Melissa asked with anticipation.

Alan read the e-mail aloud to Melissa.

Hello Alan,

I am real sorry about Mark. Unfortunately, we never got married. All I know is that he left me for San Francisco and never contacted me again. I never knew he was in Detroit. It is truly a shame for I dearly loved him. I am sorry that I do not know anymore than that and can't be of some more help to you. If you have more questions feel free to call me at (260) 555-1058.

My sincerest apologies,
Kayla Gagne

"What do you make of that, Melissa?"
"I wished she could have provided us with a clue."
"On the contrary, she did provide us with a clue."
"What?"
"We now know he left for San Francisco and didn't transfer to another campus like I previously thought."
"Okay, but she couldn't tell us anymore than that."
"Remember, Melissa, that she doesn't even know me and apparently hasn't known Mark in a few years either. It's tough to regurgitate all those memories and information into an e-mail to a complete stranger. If I got to talk to her face-to-face she might remember something else she might have forgotten. We know she lives in Indiana, because she has a Fort Wayne phone number. So let's call her and set up an interview. You feel like a drive out of state in the morning, Melissa?"
"Are you kidding, can I drive again?"
"If you can wake up before 8:00 a.m."
"Ouch. Maybe you ought to drive tomorrow then."

It was seven o'clock the next morning, and Alan was ready to go, but Melissa was still asleep. Alan, with grace, decided to crank up the stereo and put in a Billy Idol CD. Alan chose the track "Cradle of Love." The beginning beats would surly wake Melissa up. Upon hitting play, the whole room vibrated.

Melissa awakened to the deafening loud beats, moaning and groaning.
"Come on, Melissa, its 8:00 a.m., time to rock the cradle of love."
Melissa, groggy as can be said, "Ugh, it's too early."
"Yes, it is, but we have an appointment with Kayla Gagne at 10:00 a.m."
"Why can't the rest of the world sleep in like us?"
"Because we are unemployed and don't have jobs like other people. Now come on, you know I am lost without my Melissa."

Reluctantly, Melissa got up and around and got in the black Firebird with Alan. Alan put in the Billy Idol CD, got on I-69, and headed straight to Fort Wayne, Indiana.

"I called Kayla last night. She agreed to talk with us, but we had to do it in the morning. She is a nurse in the DuPont Hospital and her shift starts at 1:00 p.m."

Alan and Melissa arrived at the residence of Kayla Gagne at 10:12 a.m. Gagne lived on the northwestern end of the city. Alan rang the doorbell of the white, ranch-style house. A five-feet-two-inch tall but slightly overweight blond answered the door.

"Good morning, Kayla. I'm Alan Williams. We spoke earlier."

"Oh, yes. I have been expecting you."

"This is my girlfriend and assistant, Melissa Henneman.

Melissa said, "How do you do?"

"I'm great, thanks."

Alan, getting impatient standing around, leaning against the house and trying to stretch out his legs from the long drive said, "Well, may we come in?"

"Sure, yes. Would you like some breakfast, while you're here? You did travel a long way."

"Yes we did, and yes, breakfast would be nice." Alan was looking around the house trying to deduce any facts he could pick up on Kayla.

"What would you like to eat?"

"You wouldn't happen to have any buckwheat pancakes?"

Kayla almost laughed, "No, but we have Eggo waffles."

"No, thanks, they have high-fructose corn syrup."

Alan ate a strict diet of nothing that had high-fructose corn syrup. Alan two years ago weighed about two hundred pounds. Being only five feet eight inches tall, two hundred pounds was slightly overweight for him. Now, Alan has slimmed down to 150 pounds. Alan believed it was due by eliminating high-fructose corn syrup from his diet. According to Alan, corn syrup did nothing to control a person's hunger; in fact, it would make a person consume more and more. This, Alan conjectured, was the real reason why there was a weight problem in the United States. Alan, having a lot of time on his hands, did some research on the subject. Alan read in the *Washington Post* that a study was conducted on high-fructose corn syrup products, and half the products with high-fructose corn syrup they tested contained the element mercury. Knowing that there was a fifty-fifty chance on ingesting mercury, Alan committed not to eat high-fructose corn syrup anymore.

Kayla, thinking that Alan was some sort of control freak, tried to offer an alternative.

"Okay, would you settle for an omelet?"

"Yes, I can go with an omelet, how about you, Melissa?"

"An omelet would be good, thanks"

"Well, have a seat in the dining room, and I will be with you in ten to fifteen minutes as I make your omelets."

CHAPTER 9

"Good morning, sir," said Detective Lorenzo as she walked into Lieutenant Patrick's office.

"Lorenzo, what have you got?"

"Toxicology came back on Mark Lewis. I think you are going to want to see this."

Lieutenant Patrick opened the report and couldn't believe what he read. "If I did not know any better, I would say this is the toxicology on Sean Thomas."

"It is the same toxicology. What are the chances of that?"

"Formaldehyde, thimerosal, caustic soda, sheep's blood, we need to find out what substance has all these ingredients together and how in the hell they get into a body. Dr. Ordonez isn't getting reckless downstairs, is he?"

"On it, sir." Lorenzo said with a silly grin on her attractive face.

"Have you talked with Williams, yet?"

"No, sir."

"Well, call him and get his butt over here."

"Yes, sir. Can't wait to do that."

"Is there anything you want me to tell him in particular?"

"No, just tell him to report here as soon as possible."

In Fort Wayne, Indiana, Melissa and Alan were enjoying the hospitality provided to them by Kayla Gagne.

"Would you like milk with your omelet?" said Kayla in the kitchen.

"Is it organic?" Alan loved milk but would not drink it unless it was organic.

"No, it's not. I'm sorry."

"That's okay. I do not need anything to drink."

"Here is your omelet, then. Now you can fire away with any questions you might have."

"Well, the first thing is to thank you for taking the time to see us this morning. We never really knew each other, only through our mutual friend, Mark."

"Oh, it's no problem. Sometimes I miss Mark from time to time. Now I can put closure on this part of my life."

"You two were engaged to be married, correct?"

"Yes."

"How does someone just run off to San Francisco and break the whole thing off and not even bother to communicate?"

"I don't know, but toward the end of that final semester when you were with him in school, he fell in with a weird bunch of people."

"Weird people, who, what do you mean?"

"One time they came over to our apartment by DuPont Hospital to deliver Mark a note. I don't know who they were, but they did not look normal or act normal. They would always give me dirty, evil looks."

"You say or do something that would have warranted such provocation?"

"No, I think it was because I was a girl."

"You think they were gay?"

"Maybe. I don't know. I just thought gay people acted feminine in public and were not mean to people all the time."

"Well, you shouldn't judge a class of people based on a stereotype. Why San Francisco?"

"Because that's where all the gay people go," Melissa interjected. Both Alan and Kayla stared at Melissa for a second. Melissa immediately apologized.

"Mark told me he was going to San Francisco, but why, I could never find out. He never told me."

"Didn't you ask him, though?"

"Yes, but he said he couldn't tell. It was a secret."

"You wouldn't happen to still have the note?"

"No, Mark made sure it was destroyed immediately."

"Did you get a glance at it? Could you remember any of the words that were on it? Did it say San Francisco?"

"I barely got a glance at it. I know it didn't say San Francisco on it. The only word I can recall from it was the word 'Grove,' I think it was."

Upon hearing the word "Grove," it seemed as if a lightbulb went off in Alan's head with a lightbulb that had never been brighter.

"Of course!"

"What is it, Alan?" Melissa said. As Melissa and Kayla waited with anticipation with what Alan had figured out.

"Bohemian Grove." said Alan.

"I never heard of it." said Kayla was a bit confused.

"No doubt, many people haven't heard of Bohemian Grove," said Alan.

"Well, come on spill, Alan. What do you know?" Melissa said impatiently.

"Bohemian Grove is a secret society that meets every year in July in the Redwood Forest, just north of San Francisco. They hire gay prostitutes and have homosexual orgies.

Moans and groans came from both Melissa and Kayla. "That's sick!" shouted Kayla.

"They also run a satanic ritual called the Cremation of Care where they burn in effigy a small child as part of a sacrifice."

"Oh my God!" exclaimed Melissa.

"Now I am unsure if the sacrifice is real or just part of a mock ceremony."

"Still, that's just wrong though," said Kayla.

Alan continued, "Some of the most prominent men in the world are members of this elite club, including former U.S. Presidents Nixon, Carter, Reagan, Bush Sr., Clinton, and George W. Bush."

"No surprise on the last one." Melissa mocked.

"Wait, if it is so secret, how do you know about it, Alan? Are you a member or ex-member?" questioned Kayla.

"No, in 2000, a man from Texas successfully infiltrated inside Bohemian Grove and got out with video footage. He is the only person to have done so successfully. They have beefed up security since then. He made a documentary out of it, and I have a copy of the documentary at home."

Melissa added, "Kayla, you have to understand something about Alan. God has blessed him with a very gifted mind. How do you think he had a 3.97 grade point average in college? He got that by just studying hard? No. He has a photographic memory, and the information that is stored in that brain of his makes him a walking encyclopedia.

"Thank you, Melissa. That is the highest compliment I ever received in my life. Glad to see your finally awake now," said Alan, giving Melissa praise and adoration.

At that moment, music started playing. *I don't need your civil war . . .* It was the song "Civil War" by Guns 'N Roses.

"What's that?" asked Kayla.

"It's my cell phone," said Alan. "Alan Williams."

"Alan, where the hell are you?" said Detective Lorenzo sounding all pissed off.

"I am in Fort Wayne."

"Fort Wayne! I gave you specific instructions not to leave town, let alone leave the state!"

"Well, we are helping with your investigation, and our investigation led us to Fort Wayne, and if I recall right, which I usually do, Lieutenant Patrick said we could investigate in any manner we liked."

There was a silence at the other end for a moment before Lorenzo could figure out Alan was right again. "All right, well Lieutenant Patrick wants your butt back to Detroit as soon as possible and report with what you got in your investigation. You do have something to report back with, don't you?"

"Oh yes, we are making progress."

"Good to hear, how long before you get back?"

"We can leave right now, but it will take three to four hours to get back."

"All right, see you when you get here." Lorenzo hung up.

"Well, Kayla, it was very nice to meet you and thank you for the lovely breakfast and taking time with us. We've got to get back to Detroit."

"You're welcome, good luck in your investigation," said Kayla.

Alan and Melissa quickly hopped into their Firebird and burned rubber out of Fort Wayne.

"You never knew your friend, Mark, was part of the Bohemian Grove?" asked Melissa.

"I had no idea. I never would have guessed," answered Alan. Alan later continued explaining Bohemian Grove. "The Bohemian Club was originally created in 1872. It had intended to be an all-male drinking establishment. Now it is place where the elite and high-ranking politicians and businessmen get together and set key policies. You think laws and policies get made in Congress. Not at all, they are done at Bohemian Grove."

Melissa's brain was spinning a thousand miles an hour hearing the shocking details Alan was spilling about Bohemian Grove.

"And they perform homosexual orgies while they do this?" said Melissa.

"We can certainly deduce this, because it was confirmed that they hire male prostitutes at the Grove. News releases have said as much. They hold a mock satanic ritual called the Cremation of Care, where they burn an infant as part of a mock sacrifice. They also worship an owl. That is the Great Owl of Bohemia. The owl's name is Moloch. You have seen it before."

"I have?" Melissa said in disbelief.

"You got a dollar bill?"

"Yes."

"Get it out."

Melissa rifled through her black leather purse for her wallet and opened her greenback in front of her. "Okay, I see no owl."

"Take my magnifying glass from the glove department and look in the upper right-hand corner where the shield is. On the upper left part of the shield, there is a part of the shield that juts out in the shape of a crescent moon. The owl is right over the crescent moon."

"Oh my God, I can see it! How did you know?"

"I have been in research of things like this for a few years now."

"Well, you said every president since Carter has been there. Why has this not been reported in the news before?"

"It has been reported on C-SPAN's *Washington Journal*, but outside of that, no you're not going to hear about it on the mainstream news. You forget, Melissa, this is a secret society, and they don't want the people to know about it."

"Surely, independent media would want to tell about this if they knew?"

"Independent and alternative media, yes, would and have, because they are not owned by corporations. Bohemian Grove have some of the corporations' best interests at heart, so mainstream media, they are not going to want to tell."

"And this is all done every year in July in San Francisco?"

"Actually, it is in Monte Rio, California, which is seventy miles north of San Francisco."

"What does it mean to our murder, that Mark was a part of this cult?"

"I am not exactly sure yet, but perhaps Lorenzo can tell us something when we see her."

"Well, the next question is what are you going to say to Lorenzo? You're not going to go to her with all this or that will confirm everything she has said about you being a conspiracy theorist."

"Don't worry about Lorenzo. I know what to say to her."

In truth, Alan knew Melissa was right. Alan merely wanted to calm his girlfriend down, but Melissa brought up a good point. Alan wasn't sure what he would say to Lorenzo.

CHAPTER 10

Four hours later, Alan and Melissa made it back to Detroit and arrived in Lieutenant Patrick's office. Patrick sees Alan and Melissa in the station trying to get some help and welcomes the pair back to his office.

"Well, have you made any progress in the Thomas's case?" questioned Patrick.

"Yes, we have."

"Good. Let me get Lorenzo. Just wait here."

While Alan and Melissa were waiting, Melissa asked Alan, "What are you going to say?"

Alan whispered back, "On Thomas's murder, I am going to tell them everything, including the Freemasons. On Bohemian Grove, we are going to keep mum. Besides, we can't connect Thomas to Bohemian Grove, just Mark Lewis. We aren't supposed to be investigating the Lewis case, anyway."

Right at that moment, Alan could hear Patrick and Lorenzo down the hallway and stopped his conservation with Melissa. Alan immediately began to act like they were waiting patiently.

"What were you whispering about, Alan?" said Lorenzo inquisitively.

"Nothing!" Alan said with a big gloat on his face. Alan's face was like he was giving away his hand at a poker game.

With the expression on Alan's face, Lorenzo began to get paranoid. Lorenzo then said to Patrick, "You told them, didn't you?"

"Told me what," said Alan as the lieutenant was shaking his head.

"Well, you might as well tell him now. The cat is out of the bag," said Patrick.

Lorenzo, who couldn't bring herself to face this moment, was now forced to face it. Lorenzo took a deep breath and said, "Mark Lewis did not kill himself, he was murdered."

Alan making no reaction to the comment replied, "Well, I could have told you that. Oh wait, I did tell you that."

"Okay, can we stop?" said Lorenzo, not in the mood to start a fight.

"Yes, I'm sorry. Let's all try to cooperate with one another and solve these murders, which is what I have been trying to do in the first place," Alan said.

"All right, tell us what you got, Alan," said Patrick.

"The murder of Sean Thomas was the work of Freemasons."

"Freemasons, I thought it was the work of a satanic cult," said Patrick.

"Actually it is, but let me explain."

"You know, you are talking to a Freemason," Patrick interrupted.

"Well, may I ask what degree you are?"

"First degree."

"Then, you should know the oath you had to swear to obtain that first degree."

"I am not allowed to talk about it."

"Think, Lieutenant, though. Don't you see the connection, sir?

There were a few moments of silence before Alan continued. "Let me read the oath to you, then. The oath says, 'Binding myself under no less penalty than that of having my throat cut across, my tongue torn out by its roots, and my body buried in the rough sands of the sea, at low-water mark, where the tide ebbs and flows in twenty-four hours, should I ever knowingly violate this my Entered Apprentice obligation.'"

"Oh my God, Lieutenant, he's right," said Lorenzo with astonishment.

"I guess I have been blind as a beetle," stated Patrick.

"That's all right, Lieutenant. It happens to the best of us," said Alan.

"So the killer is a Freemason. What do we do about it?" questioned the lieutenant.

"Well, not only our killer, but our victim also is, as well. We need to find the lodge that Thomas attended and find out everyone who attends his lodge."

"How do we do that, Alan? The Masonic Temple isn't simply going to let the police in and allow us to do that, and as you so repeatedly said so many times in school, you need probable cause to conduct a search and obtain a warrant," said Lorenzo, lecturing Alan again. "No judge is going to sign off on a warrant with what we've got so far."

"Lorenzo, for once your right." replied Alan. "We won't need a warrant though."

"We don't need a warrant! Alan, are you feeling all right, baby?" said Melissa, concerned.

"We don't need a warrant, if we have our very own Freemason to help us out, if you get where I am going with this."

"Oh, no. Are you kidding, Alan?" said Patrick getting worried.

"Bear with me, Lieutenant, and hear me out. How many lodges are there in the Detroit Masonic Temple?"

"There are nine."

"Nine, okay. Lieutenant, was Thomas ever in one of your lodge meetings?"

"No, I think I would have known, Alan."

"Which lodge do you attend?"

"The Detroit lodge."

"All right, we know it is not the Detroit Lodge, so that's one down and eight to go. Lieutenant, if you would go attend the other eight lodge meetings and find which lodge knew Sean Thomas, then find out the people present at that meeting, you will have a list of suspects."

"But that may take a month, don't the Freemasons have their meeting once a month?" commented Lorenzo.

"Actually it will only take a week," replied Alan.

"A week?" Lorenzo stunned by the response.

"In the Detroit area, all the Freemasons meet in the first week of the month, which starts on Monday, correct, Lieutenant?"

"Yes, that's correct."

"Then, Lieutenant, will you do it? Nobody else will be able to get inside, because they're not a Freemason. Come on, it's a little bit of social engineering, but you can handle it."

"Okay, but what will you be doing during this time?"

"Lorenzo and I will spend some quality time together to solve the murder of my friend, Mark Lewis."

"What! No, please, Lieutenant, don't make me work with him. He was bad enough to me as a student. Don't make me partner with him," cried Lorenzo in horror.

The lieutenant was amused with the thought and said, "Actually, I think that will be a great idea, since I will be sweating it out at these Freemason meetings, this will give something to look forward to when this week is over. You two have fun and try not kill each other." Lorenzo grimaced in agony at the decision made by her superior. "Lorenzo, take Alan and Melissa downstairs and show them what you found in Lewis's personal effects. Oh, but before you all go, toxicology came back on Lewis.

"What does it say?" asked Alan with intrigue in his voice.

"The same crap that was in Thomas's body, the formaldehyde, the thimerosal, caustic soda, sheep's blood, and the rest of it, was also found in Lewis. Coincidence?"

"Well, you know what I say, Lorenzo?" asked Alan.

"Yeah, yeah, that there are no such things as coincidence, only the illusion of coincidence, blah, blah, blah, God, I feel like I am back in school again," said Lorenzo already knowing what Alan was going to say.

"Well, it's from *V for Vendetta*," said Alan.

"Yeah, I know you constantly talked about in your papers for class. By the way, I hated that movie."

"Gee, wouldn't have been able to deduce that," replied Alan.

"Shut up!" Lorenzo screeched back to Alan.

CHAPTER 11

Walking downstairs into the morgue, everyone felt, including Melissa, awkward at the fact that the trio would have to work together on the Lewis's murder. An eerie silence fell upon the trio as they entered the morgue.

"The personal effects of Mark Lewis, please," requested Detective Lorenzo. "We found a few things on him. Hopefully one of his items will give us a lead."

Lorenzo started to go through the bag of items and one by one placed them on a counter. The first thing Lorenzo pulled out was a wallet. The wallet was a black leather bifold. Nothing too strange or out of the ordinary with that. He had about a hundred dollars on him, a couple of credit cards, identification, a business card, and membership cards.

"Let me see the membership cards?" asked Alan.

The membership cards consisted of an AAA card, membership to Barnes & Noble bookstore, and another card with an owl with the letter B and C on either side of the owl in the top right corner.

"Bohemian Club member," said Alan.

"What is the Bohemian Club?" asked Lorenzo.

"Now that you're on the case you better know the whole truth."

"The truth about what?"

"The Bohemian Club," Alan paused before finishing his sentence to Lorenzo, "is a secret society that meets every year in July in the redwood forest, just north of San Francisco. They hire gay prostitutes and have homosexual orgies."

"You've been there?" asked Lorenzo strangely.

"No, never been there. They would not want me. Anyway, they are very particular about whom they want, and they would certainly throw my ass out."

"President Bush is welcomed there, though," Melissa interjected.

"Melissa, I love you, but now is not the time," whispered Alan.

Lorenzo, with a dumbfounded look on her face, said, "Uh-huh, I see. So are you saying this Bohemian Club is directly involved with our murder?"

Alan responded, "I don't know yet. Chances are they are, though. What else do you have?"

Next, Lorenzo pulled out an appointment log. "This is an appointment log Lewis has made to keep track of appointments with a Dr. Eric Leyland, apparently that was Lewis's physician; State Rep. Tony Kiebler, that is the local congressman in Detroit; Andy Woolery, TV anchorman for the local news; and his girlfriend's name Casey, which we don't have a last name for yet."

Alan and Melissa were stunned by the fact that Mark had a girlfriend. Alan asked, "How do you know it's his girlfriend?"

"He's got hearts written over and by her name. What else would you call it?" said Lorenzo

"I have to say, that it's cruel by Mark to treat Kayla the way he did, then to turn around and see another girl," Melissa chimed in with her opinion. "I thought he was your friend, Alan."

Alan seemed to be puzzled by this fact. "Either he has radically changed in three years, I never knew him at all, or something is not right with this."

"Or something is not right with him, which provided somebody a motive to kill him," said Lorenzo.

"I would like to interview all those guys in his appointment log," Alan requested.

"Of course, I will get their information, and we will see them first thing in the morning," Lorenzo responded.

"Uggggh. Not another early start," moaned Melissa.

"Afraid so," said Alan. "What were his appointments for the day of the murder?"

"Just a meeting with the state rep," responded Lorenzo.

"For what time and where?"

"10:30 a.m. at the Ramada Inn."

"Well, that gives us something to work on."

"Hell, that gives us a prime suspect," said Lorenzo.

"Easy, Lorenzo. Lewis met his death between noon and twelve thirty. That still leaves with an hour or two in the timeline where we still don't know what happened."

"Well, he is still the closest thing to a suspect that we got."

"Well, if there is nothing else to show, is there anything we can do, before the day is over?"

"No, go home, get some sleep. I want your butts here at 8:00 a.m. sharp, no excuses."

"All right, Lorenzo. Have a good night."

As Alan and Melissa drove back to Jackson, Melissa asked, "What are you going to do tonight?"

"I need to go back and watch that Bohemian Grove documentary again. I feel I am missing something, and it is nagging at me. I feel Bohemian Grove is involved in this somehow."

"Do you have any idea who this new girlfriend of Mark is?"

"No idea. No worries, I've got confidence I'll know soon enough."

CHAPTER 12

Melissa and Alan arrived in their digs later that same evening. Both were extremely exhausted from all the time driving on the road, nearly eleven hours worth. They just wanted to kick back and relax.

"You want me to fire up the Bohemian Grove DVD?" asked Melissa.

"Yeah. Oh, I forgot you haven't seen it yet. I have to warn you, it is nothing like *Smokey and the Bandit*." responded Alan.

"I figured as much, but what the hell, it could still be entertaining."

Melissa was shocked to see well-known politicians dress up in red, white, and black robes carrying torches. "It looks like a KKK meeting," blurted out Melissa. In a particular scene in the documentary, the infiltrators are in the parking lot, and a beige jeep with a Bohemian Club logo drives and picks up the 'infiltrators' to drive them inside the grove. "Pause it, Melissa!" shouted Alan, nearly scaring the living daylights out of his girlfriend.

"What is it, Alan?"

"The driver, I have seen him before." Alan got up around the room acting like he has the answer right in front of him but doesn't know what he has got. "Melissa, I have seen that man before, but I can't place where I have seen him. Melissa, you go on and watch the rest of the film, I am going out to be alone and try to remember where I have seen him."

Melissa acknowledged and watched the rest of the film. Melissa got to see parts of the forest where Bohemian Grove is located. Then she got to watch the Cremation of Care in its entirety. Melissa was both apathetic and feeling nauseous, but couldn't help to watch all the way through. The unusualness of it overcame her. It was like watching a bad opera play.

Just then, Alan bolted out into the room and shouted, "Casey Thomas, the driver is Casey Thomas."

"Oh my God, you're right," Melissa surprised to learn another piece of the puzzle. "So both victims were members of Bohemian Grove. Is someone trying to kill off members of the club?"

Alan, pacing around the room, took time to think about what the new implications he had uncovered meant. "Detective Lorenzo said that Mark had a girlfriend name Casey, you know hearts around the name in his planner. What if Casey was the name of his boyfriend?"

"You mean Mark's boyfriend was Casey Thomas?"

"Yes, Melissa, now think about it. Both were members of the Bohemian Grove, a homosexual club. They had to have known each other from each visit that is made every July. They probably got extra friendly toward one another. I think our murders are related now."

"But how?"

"I don't know the reason yet, but our murderer has to be a Freemason and a Bohemian Grove member."

"Well, that shouldn't be too hard, right. I mean there can't be that many around."

"None who are going to publicly admit it."

"What are you going to do, Alan?"

"We don't worry about that now. Right now, we need to find a suspect. We need to interview every one of Mark's contacts that he wrote in his planner. It happens to be that we have a nine o'clock interview with State Representative Kiebler. The last person we know to have seen Mark Lewis alive."

"Oh, I hate getting up early. Incidentally, Alan, thank you so much for letting me watch *Bohemian Grove*. It was like watching the thug cult from *Indiana Jones and the Temple of Doom* with old, ugly, and disgusting men giving off an orgasm to a burning human sacrifice. Remind me not to let you pick the movie again next time."

CHAPTER 13

This morning, Melissa got up reluctantly, because did not want to give Alan another opportunity to rudely awaken her like he did the day before. As Lorenzo ordered, Alan and Melissa arrived in her office at 8:00 a.m. sharp.

"Well, Alan, one thing I can say about you is that you are punctual," remarked Lorenzo.

"Well, I believe this is the only time you ever have complimented on me on anything," responded Alan. "I learned something last night and I have to show you."

"Well, spill it Alan."

"Do you have a DVD player?"

"Downstairs, next to the forensics lab. We've got some time before the interview with Kiebler."

"Okay then, fire it up."

"What have you got there, Alan?"

"This is a documentary and footage taken at the Bohemian Grove in July 2000." Alan hands the DVD to Lorenzo. Lorenzo takes the DVD, not sure where Alan is going with it.

"Wait, this is the same place you said President Bush goes, and they hold homosexual orgies?"

"The same."

"You have footage!?"

"Yes."

"So, it is real after all."

"When will you believe me, Lorenzo? Now, this is what I want you to see."

"A parking lot?"

"Wait for it . . . and . . . now pause it."

"What am I looking for?"

"Look at the driver. Haven't you seen him somewhere before?"

Lorenzo opens up the case files to see the photograph of the dead Casey Thomas. She looks back at the monitor to make sure.

"It's Casey Thomas."

"Very good, Lorenzo. You're not totally useless."

Lorenzo smirks back at Alan with a dirty look. Lorenzo was thinking how much more she would have to put up with Alan and his arrogance.

"Now, yesterday you told me that Mark had a girlfriend name Casey, because he had hearts over the name. What if it wasn't a girlfriend, but his gay lover Casey Thomas?"

"Come on, Alan, that is a bit of a stretch, don't you think? I mean the guy is like fifteen years older than Mark."

"What, people don't date people fifteen years apart? It's been known to happen."

"Well, I don't buy it."

"May I remind you that you are the one who also said that the Lewis death was a suicide. Anyway, how do you explain that two murders and both of the victims are members of Bohemian Grove? Just coincidence?"

"I don't know. I never heard of Bohemian Grove until yesterday. Let's go, I'll take you to see Rep. Kiebler. We are meeting him in half an hour."

CHAPTER 14

Detective Lorenzo drove Alan and Melissa downtown Detroit. Representative Kiebler had an office in that area. Alan and Melissa were so thankful Lorenzo drove. Neither of them liked to drive in downtown Detroit. It seemed like a chore to drive when they wanted to get to a Tigers game. They walked in the office, finding Representative Kiebler talking with his secretary. Kiebler stood about six feet one inch, weighed about 180 pounds, with some gray showing in his hair. He looked like CNN's Anderson Cooper's younger brother. Kiebler turned around and greeted Lorenzo.

"Good morning, you must be Detective Lorenzo. My secretary alerted me that you would be coming today."

"Yes, that's correct. This is Alan Williams. He is assisting me on the case."

Kiebler greeted him, saying, "How do you do?"

"And this is my assistant, Melissa Henneman."

"Wow, everybody's got an assistant these days. Let's step into my office."

Lorenzo, Alan, and Melissa stepped into the Representative's office. It was well-refined and had a presidential feel.

"Well, what can I help you with?" questioned Kiebler.

Lorenzo led the questioning. "We are investigating the murder of Mark Lewis in his hotel room from a couple of days ago."

"Murder, but I thought the newspaper said it was a suicide."

Lorenzo looked to Alan as if she would never hear the end of it. Lorenzo spoke quickly through her next sentence. "The paper got it wrong, so how did you know Mark Lewis?"

"Mark was interested in politics or at least working in it. He came to me wanting a position on my staff. See, I have aspirations of making it to

Washington D.C. and I am going to need staff people to keep my political career on track if I want to make it to the big time."

"You met him in the hotel room on the day in question. What did you have to talk about?"

Kiebler looked stunned the police already knew about the meeting.

"Uh . . . yeah, I was there to tell Mark that he was hired. Isn't it ironic, that he met his fate after I left?"

"When did you leave the hotel?"

"I left the hotel about 11:15 a.m."

"So you were there about forty-five minutes in his room, just to tell Mark he was hired?"

"Well, I also went over his staff position and what some of his duties would be, answered questions he had."

"When you left Mark's room and the hotel, did you see anything suspicious?"

"No, I am sorry. I wish I could be more helpful."

"Where did you go after you left the hotel?"

"Back here into my office."

"How long?"

"For a few hours, I had some work to catch up on."

"Someone can verify you being here at that time?"

"My secretary, just ask her if you need confirmation."

"Question, Mr. Kiebler," Alan interrupted. "I knew Mark, and he was never interested in politics. He was interested in WWE wrestling and watching the Dallas Cowboys. You want me to believe that he came to you for a job to work in politics?"

"I mean how can I answer that? Maybe you didn't know Mark like you thought you did."

"Just before you arrived in his room, Mark phoned me to ask for my help, but he didn't tell me what he needed help with. Do you have any idea what he needed help with?"

"No, he seemed all right to me when I talked to him, especially when I told him he was hired."

Alan, frustrated that he was not getting anywhere with this interview, decided to cut his losses and move on to the next interview. "Thanks, Mr. Kiebler for allowing us to take up so much of your valuable time." With that, Alan and Melissa quickly got outside. To Alan, it was like a breath of fresh air.

Melissa acted a little concerned, "Baby, are you all right?"

"We didn't get anything out of this guy."

"You know he was lying?"

"I don't know. I just know we didn't get a clue from him."

Lorenzo finally met up with Alan and Melissa outside Kiebler's office. "The secretary can confirm. Mr. Kiebler was in his office between noon and twelve thirty. Looks like his alibi checks out."

Alan, not at all surprised, "Yeah, that secretary is the type that would cover his ass anyway."

"You think they're lying?" responded Lorenzo.

"I don't know, forget it. Who's our next interview with?" said Alan, agitated. Alan had a natural distrust for politicians in general. Alan thinks they are all liars, but the trick was proving it to Lorenzo, which he couldn't do at this time.

"Andy Woolery is our next person to interview," stated Lorenzo.

"All right, maybe we will have better luck with him. Let's just get the hell out of here."

CHAPTER 15

Andy Woolery, TV news anchorman for the local news in Detroit. Woolery was fifty-two years old, brown hair, slim figure, still had good looks for the camera. Woolery had been reporting on the news every night for the last twenty years in Detroit. Most people would know who he was from watching television. Alan, Melissa, and Lorenzo drove to his residence, which was in the suburb of Franklin. Lorenzo rang the doorbell to Woolery's two-story house.

"Andy Woolery, Detective Lorenzo, homicide. This is Alan Williams and Melissa Henneman, their assisting me with the case."

"Uh, yes, how can I help you, Detective?" said Woolery who seemed somewhat apprehensive but calm at the same time.

"We are investigating the murder of Mark Lewis in the Ramada Inn, a couple of days ago."

"Oh, yeah, I remember that, but we reported it as a suicide."

Detective Lorenzo, unable to live it down, carried on with her questions.

"Yes, we know. We were . . . too quick to jump to that conclusion. What we would like to ask you is how you knew Mark Lewis?"

"I didn't," responded Woolery.

"Well, that's interesting, because Mark Lewis knew you."

"Well, that's nothing, everyone in this city knows me. I am live on their television sets at six o'clock every night."

"Yeah, but not too many keep your name in their planner as one of their contacts. Care to explain?"

"Okay, okay. I wasn't lying when I said I didn't know Mark Lewis. I never met the man." Alan and Lorenzo looked at each other as if they were slightly puzzled with Woolery's answer. "He has been phoning me the last few weeks, telling me he had a big story he wanted to break to me, in front of the world. I said sure, what is it? Well, he wouldn't tell me over the phone.

He was too afraid his phone was being wiretapped. Now, I guess we'll never know what secret he was hiding."

"Why didn't you ask to meet with him in person?" asked Lorenzo.

"I did, but he said he wouldn't make that drastic of a move until he was ready."

"Did it sound like he was in fear of his life?"

"Yes, it did."

"When was the last time he phoned you?"

"It would have been three days ago."

"What did he say in the last conservation you had with him?"

"He said he wanted to meet with me but did not want to discuss any details of the meeting over the phone, for fear of being compromised. Since this didn't help me, he said he was going to come up with an idea to send a message to me where it could not be intercepted."

"That was it?"

"He wouldn't talk any further than that."

Detective Lorenzo, always suspicious of details, asked Woolery, "Okay, would you mind telling me where you were between noon and twelve thirty during the day in question?"

"I was here, home alone."

"Do you have anyone here that can testify to you being here?"

"No, surely you don't think I have anything to do with this murder. I never met the man, for Christ's sake."

"Thank you, Mr. Woolery. We might be in touch later."

With that, Lorenzo walked Melissa and Alan back to her red Chevrolet Impala.

"Well, what do you think, Alan? You're awfully quiet," Lorenzo asked Alan.

"I believe him."

"Do you? I thought his story was hokey to me."

"I think every story you hear is hokey to you, Lorenzo. Now, think about it, it makes sense. When Mark phoned me that morning, I got the same feelings as Mr. Woolery just described. Mark did not want to talk much and discuss too many details over the phone. The secret that Mark was hiding is the reason that he called me. Mark was in fear for his life. Obviously, it was justified, look at the result. We must know what he was hiding."

"So what do you want to do now, Alan?"

"Well, let's talk with Mark's personal physician, Dr. Eric Leyland. Maybe we'll get lucky the secret is confided with his doctor."

CHAPTER 16

An hour later, Lorenzo, Alan, and Melissa were sitting in the lobby of the office of one Dr. Eric Leyland. "The doctor will be with you as soon as he is done with a patient," beckoned the receptionist. While the trio was waiting for the doctor to come out, the nurses were arguing among themselves over who misplaced a certain file. Alan whispered to Melissa, "Have you ever noticed how all doctor office workers are on top of their jobs?" The trio could barely get the words of nurses that were questioning the filing system, "More than three years . . . have to update the computer . . . throw the file out." Alan whispered again, "Sounds like Dr. Leyland does not have much support in the support staff."

Just then, an overweight middle-aged woman waddled down the narrow hallway into the lobby to grab her jacket that was hanging on the rack by the door. An elderly, chubby man, five feet six inches tall in a white lab coat walked with her. "Don't forget to call us on Saturday to confirm your scheduled flu shot with us," said the elderly man in the white lab coat. "Good day," the elderly man dismissed the middle aged woman leaving the office. Lorenzo got up and inquired if the elderly man was Dr. Leyland.

"Excuse me, Dr. Leyland?"

"Yes, I'm Dr. Leyland."

"Detective Sara Lorenzo, Detroit Homicide."

"What is this about?"

"We're investigating the death of Mark Lewis. I believe you were his doctor."

"Yes, I was. You probably would like his medical records. My staff can get that for you."

"That's fine," Lorenzo said abruptly, but we would like a few minutes of your time, if you don't mind, sir. We have a few questions we hope to ask you."

"And who is we?"

"Oh! I'm sorry. This is Alan Williams, a private investigator and his assistant, Melissa Henneman."

"I don't understand. Why bring in a private investigator over a suicide?"

On that remark, Alan chimed in, "Because we are talking about murder, not suicide. Please, wouldn't you rather talk about this in your office and not in front of your patients in the waiting room?"

"Right this way, then."

Dr. Leyland led Lorenzo, Alan, and Melissa down a narrow hall that could not have been more than four feet wide, with dull and dreary gray carpeting. They went about fifteen feet down, then turn around the left corner into Leyland's office. Inside the room, there was a regal and elegant feel. The carpet was blood red. The lower half part of the walls were a very dark brown with wood siding. The upper half of the wall was painted a cream color. On the back wall, immediately upon entering, was what could easily be mistaken for a crucifix, at first glance. The kind of crucifix you would see on the altars of big Catholic cathedrals or basilicas. Then you look at it some more and you see it is not a crucifix, but a giant caduceus.

Both Lorenzo and Melissa said "Jesus" at the same time. "No, it is not Jesus, just the symbol of our profession. Not too many come in here, but anyone who has, usually mistakes my caduceus for a crucifix. I take my profession very seriously."

Alan, having the encyclopedia in his brain, got inquisitive and had to ask the doctor, "Why is the caduceus the symbol of the medical profession?"

"It's from the Old Testament. In the book of Exodus, when Moses was fleeing Egypt, he was directed by God to make a pole upon which he was to place a snake on it made of bronze. When it was looked upon, this symbol would spare the lives of the Israelites who were stricken by venomous snake bites."

"Yeah, but you're using the symbol as a symbol of medicine. In 4000 BC, the Greeks used the Rod of Asclepius as their symbol of medicine. Aren't you confusing the caduceus with the Rod of Asclepius, which only has one snake and no wings?"

"There are some doctors who use the Rod of Asclepius as the symbol of the medical profession. However, because of my Jewish beliefs, I choose to use this symbol of the caduceus."

"Aren't these the same doctors as well who say that Hermes was the god who leads the dead to the underworld? Is he not only associated with wealth and commerce, but also the patron of thieves? Doctor, does it not make sense to you, then, that you would not want to associate yourself with such trickery, death, and the accumulation of wealth?"

Upon hearing those last words, the doctor's facial expression became so tense; you could cut the tension in the room up with a knife. You could easily tell Dr. Leyland was unhappy with the implication of Alan's question along with the tone he used in the context of his question. Dr. Leyland's dark brown eyes fixed upon Alan in a way that if looks could kill, Alan would be spread out over the floor with his blood poured out from every orifice and splattered over his entire body, matching the carpet.

Dr. Leyland's tone changed dramatically. "Get the hell out of my office!" bellowed Dr. Leyland. "GET THE HELL OUT NOW!" the doctor screamed louder.

Immediately, Sara Lorenzo, expecting a fight to break out, spoke up, "All right, that's enough! Alan, wait in the car."

"But we are not done yet."

"No, you're done. Now wait in the car."

Melissa, always thinking discretion is the better part of valor, took Alan back to the car.

"Baby, what wrong?"

"Melissa, that guy is evil, I know it."

"I found his office creepy if that is what you mean?"

"No, it's more than that. The caduceus is an Illuminati symbol. The fact that he is in love with it like it was his god has got satanic cult written all over. You even mistook it for the crucifixion. A Christian having a big crucifixion on his wall would make sense. He tried to tie in his Jewish faith with the caduceus. They have nothing to do with each other. I don't believe it.

"Don't believe what?"

"That he is Jewish."

Melissa and Alan waited for a few minutes before Lorenzo would make it back to them. Lorenzo stormed out of the office walking very briskly.

"Now, what the hell was all that about, Alan?"

"You couldn't tell I didn't like the guy?"

"Why? Because he has a big ass caduceus or whatever you call it. I don't know what you were trying to prove in there, but that was totally unprofessional and the reason why you can't land a job and the reason you are stuck with your private practice."

"You don't find anything odd about that?"

"I found it creepy, but that is no excuse to go loony and lose control. How does that little tirade of yours get us anywhere in our investigation?"

"Well, I think I have found my prime suspect."

"What, just based on his big caduceus? You have played out this conspiracy theory game one too many times now."

"No, it's not just the caduceus."

"Then what, Alan?" responded Lorenzo.

"I don't know, I am still missing something."

Lorenzo then wanted to chime in with her advice. "You know, I think Mark Lewis would be disappointed in you. Here you are, you are supposed to be solving his murder and yet you're turning his investigation into your crusade to prove that a conspiracy exists in this country. You have got to learn to trust some of those who hold authority positions. Why do you want to make everything about a conspiracy?"

Alan could not think of anything to say. Melissa wanted to say something, because she stuck by Alan the whole time believing in him on all things conspiracy. She couldn't because her head was so dizzy from the talk of Greek mythology, a subject completely foreign to her. Lorenzo sensed that the pair had been worn out from their day's investigation.

Lorenzo spoke again, "Look, I can't say you have been totally unhelpful. You really helped us out in the early stages. You knew Mark's death was a murder and not a suicide, and helped us get on the right track. Come on, let's call it a day. I will buy you both dinner tonight. What do you say? Are you okay with that?

Alan and Melissa both accepted Lorenzo's gracious invitation.

CHAPTER 17

Sergeant Lorenzo asked where Melissa and Alan would like to eat. Lorenzo already had a feeling that this would be a tall order, for she knew that Alan was very particular and stubborn about the places he eats.

"I know you don't like McDonald's, so I won't even ask, how about Red Lobster?" asked Lorenzo.

"I can't, I have a food intolerance to fish," answered Alan.

"You have a what?

"Food intolerance. It is where the body doesn't have the enzymes needed to digest a certain food properly."

"Oh, I thought a conspiracy was going to come in somewhere."

"Well, there is still a chance of getting mercury from all the pollution in our waters caused by corporations."

"Aha! I knew you couldn't resist."

"So, it's some sort of conspiracy when the CDC has admitted that as many as 4 million cases of salmonella poisoning can happen in any given year, along with 20,000 cases of E. coli contamination."

"Okay, I am sorry I asked because I know you're not going to stop. Where do you want to eat then?"

"I don't know, oh, Melissa what is that one karaoke bar we went to on the west side of Detroit?"

"River of Sticks," answered Melissa.

"Yeah, that's it. Thanks, Melissa. Sticks, Sara, do know where we are talking about it?"

"Yeah, I know the place. I guess that will be all right."

A half hour later, Lorenzo drove to a tavern on the western side of the Detroit. The tavern is located near the railroad tracks that run across the entire state of Michigan. Inside the tavern, it looked very much like a smoky pool hall from the '80s. The building was made of brick with two-level tiers.

Each tier had five pool tables, and they were all to one side of the floor. The other half of the room was a typical bar with a mahogany bar and booths to the side. Melissa, Alan, and Lorenzo walked inside and took a seat. Music was pumping through the brick structure. It was the pulsating rhythms of Rihanna's song "Disturbia." At first, Melissa thought it was just a disc jockey, but then she noticed a blackboard on the wall. The blackboard said that it was karaoke night. Karaoke always excited Melissa.

"Hey, Alan, did you know it's karaoke night?"

"Well, imagine that. How fortunate for us."

"Us?" Lorenzo wasn't sure what Alan meant.

"Alan is a karaoke master. It's where I met him in Jackson," chimed Melissa with a certain glow that was infallible about Melissa. "What are you going to sing, Alan?"

"Well, Melissa, I think we have to greet Sergeant Lorenzo to a little *East Bound and Down.*"

Lorenzo, a bit shocked, said, "Are you serious? I kind of want to discuss a few points in this case with you, and you want to torture me with karaoke!"

"You never know, karaoke might clear this case up for us. You'd be surprised how my singing gives a positive vibe and spirit to the people and the atmosphere."

"I don't believe this shit," responded Lorenzo in usual pessimistic manner toward Alan.

A waitress named Ashleigh, with similar hair to Melissa but a few inches shorter, a somewhat dark complexion, the type of skin where you couldn't tell if she is a natural olive or someone who has been in the tanning booth too long, asked for everyone to order drinks. Alan ordered his usual, which was a Smirnoff Ice. Melissa ordered Captain Morgan rum, and Lorenzo ordered a Pepsi.

Since everybody knew what they wanted to eat, the waitress took the orders immediately. Alan ordered a hamburger with mustard and mayonnaise. The waitress asked if Alan would like ketchup with his hamburger. Alan responded by telling her that ketchup has high-fructose corn syrup and that he would have none of it. Lorenzo just shook her head the whole time at Alan's eccentricity with the waitress. Melissa ordered a chicken sandwich, and Lorenzo order a cheeseburger with everything on it, just to show up Alan. The waitress was finally done and went back to the bar.

"All right, Alan, let's get back to our murder here. I think it is the congressman."

Alan rebutted back, "I think we should stay on the doctor."

Lorenzo, continuing the debate, "Okay, Alan, now think about this logically. I've got the congressman as the last person seeing our victim alive. For all we know, he could have lied about his timeline. What do you have, an old, creepy guy with a big caduceus? I think I win this time."

"What you say about the congressman is possible, but you're wrong about the doctor. I have a person who was unwilling to answer any of our questions and all around defensive."

"Well, maybe he would not have to be if you weren't so damn pushy and trite."

"You think I was trite, eh? I am not afraid to speak what is on my mind. As long as I am telling the truth, I do not see anything wrong with that. It is my First Amendment right is it not?"

"No one knows half the stuff you know, so it is going to come across that you are way out in left field. No one is going to take you seriously."

"Oh, I bet the doctor knew what I was talking about."

"Even if you're right, we do not have a lead, and the doctor is certainly not going to talk to you anymore nor me, not without an attorney present. What do you suggest we do?"

Just then the disc jockey boomed his voice into a microphone and shouted, "Alan, come on up."

"Lorenzo, I admit I do not know what the next step is and I wouldn't know what to do myself if I was in your position, but I am going to sing right now."

"Oh fine, yeah, that's just great," Lorenzo said in disgust.

As soon as the music started, and Alan started singing the first line, "East bound and down, loaded up and trucking," you could feel some electricity go through the room. Alan was like a southern Baptist minister preaching a sermon to his congregation. Alan paced around the floor, never looking at the screen to follow the words of the song. Then like the tabernacle choir, a chorus of clapping was thundering from the patrons of the bar. The room was getting into it, and they liked what they were hearing. Melissa was especially getting into it, of course. It was the point in the song where it was the last verse. Alan, without missing a beat, was singing, when an extraordinary event happened.

Alan was singing, and as he was hitting the line, "just put that hammer down and give it hell" with his arm fist pumped into the air, right at the word "hell," a woman, who looked into her midtwenties was clutching at herself like she couldn't breathe. She was also walking stiff as a board when she collapsed right at Alan's feet. The song stopped. Alan went to check on the woman who was lying on his feet. She was dead upon hitting the floor.

CHAPTER 18

Melissa and Lorenzo were immediately up from their seats to check on the dead woman. "She's dead," Alan told his partners. Lorenzo called 911. "Yes, this is Sergeant Lorenzo from Detroit Homicide. I've got a suspicious death at the River of Sticks. A woman in her midtwenties collapsed for no apparent reason. She is lying in the middle of the dance floor. Send Dr. Ordonez if you would, please, thank you."

Alan recognized the name Ordonez. Ordonez was a guest lecturer at his college. Alan was quite impressed with his talk and remembered learning a lot from his short visit. Alan will never forget how Ordonez lectured about determining the time of death and the importance of it in an investigation. One test question Alan remembered studying for was that the body cools 1 to 1.5 degrees per hour after death. In this case, everyone knows the time of death for the unfortunate woman in the bar, at least the ones that were sober and paying attention. It amazed Alan how some of the patrons were unaffected by the woman's sudden death. They just continued living in their own little world like nothing had happen.

"Dr. Ordonez works for you?" Alan said with some surprise.

"Yes, you know him?

"Ordonez is a good man. I saw him guest lecture at my college. I was quite impressed."

Lorenzo said, "I am not shocked. I can tell you two think alike."

Melissa, staring at the body, said, "What do you think she died of?"

"Well, if you ask me, I think she died from Alan's singing," Lorenzo came with a pithy response.

"What are you talking about, Lorenzo? My man was fantastic."

Alan decided to interrupt before a catfight was to ensue. "Um . . . Lorenzo, shouldn't you interview some patrons, get the identity of the victim, find out who she is and where she was coming from? All that good stuff, you know. Melissa and I will guard the body and make the sure the scene is undisturbed until forensics gets here."

Lorenzo went over to the table where the young woman's party was. There was a party of two other girls. Both of them looked in their twenties as well. One woman has curly black hair. She had a medium built to her. The other woman was a tall and lengthy blonde. "I am sorry for what happened. I am Sergeant Lorenzo, Detroit Homicide. Did you know that woman?"

The medium built woman spoke, "Yes, she was a roommate and friend of ours."

"What was her name?"

"Tiffany Burton."

"What does Tiffany do for a living?"

"We all go to school at Eastern Michigan University. We live on campus in Wise Hall."

"What was she studying?"

"Her major's in education. She had plans to be a teacher."

"Incidentally, what are your names?"

The blond said her name was Chrystal Taylor and the medium-built girl said her name was Nancy Saban.

"What time did you arrive here at the River of Sticks?"

"We got here around 5:00 p.m."

"Where did you come from before coming here to the River of Sticks?"

"We picked up Tiffany at the Walgreens in Ann Arbor. She was getting a flu shot."

"And what time would this have been?"

"Oh, this must have around four thirty.

"Did Tiffany show any signs of physical discomfort since that time?"

"No, we had no idea anything was wrong."

"What did she have to drink here?"

"She had a Bud Light."

"And what food did she order?"

"She had this bacon cheeseburger and french fries."

"I am going to ask you not to touch or get rid of any of this food. I am going to collect it for evidence."

"You think the food was tainted?"

"Right now, it is too early to determine what happened. It is very possible the food might have been tainted, but it could be anything at this point. If

I need more information, I contact you in your dorm. I think that is all I need from you, so you're free to go."

Lorenzo went back to where Alan and Melissa were protecting the body. "The victim's name is Tiffany Burton. She was an education major at the Eastern Michigan University. She lived on campus. She has two associates Chrystal Taylor and Nancy Saban; they were her friends and roommates. What do you think happened here, Alan?"

"I don't know, but it is a capital mistake to theorize before data. You know who said that, Lorenzo?"

"Uhmmm . . . *V for Vendetta*."

"No, Sherlock Holmes. But now we can get some data because Dr. Ordonez has just arrived.

"Good evening, Lorenzo." Dr. Ordonez saw Melissa and Alan and was unsure as to what they were doing with Lorenzo. "Who is with you in this investigation?" asked Dr. Ordonez.

"Oh, forgive me. This is Alan Williams and his assistant, Melissa Henneman. They were helping me on another case when this startling and unanticipated death happened right in front of us."

"Well, why do you need me then? You saw the whole thing, right?"

"Actually we are unsure what happened, we don't even know the cause of death."

Melissa interjected, "Alan was singing "East Bound and Down," and this girl fell dead right at Alan's feet."

"Really?" said Dr. Ordonez.

"If I may interrupt as well," said Alan, "I would suggest a full autopsy on this one, complete with toxicology.

"Why do you think that, Alan?" questioned Lorenzo.

"Because anytime you have a suspicious death, no matter how remote, an autopsy should be done. In fact, I think it should mandated by law!" said Alan adamantly.

Lorenzo did not disagree. "I don't disagree with that Alan. In fact, I do think it is a good idea. We have part of her dinner that is going to be taken to forensics to see if the food was tainted or poisoned, but if we come up with nothing from that, it is vital to know the cause of death. It is vital to know that anyway. We do operate efficiently from time to time, Alan. Doctor, please continue."

"Right, well, you already established the time of death. You don't need me for that. This is one of the warmest bodies I have ever worked with.

"Ewww! That's sick, Dr. Ordonez, the way you just said that," gasped Melissa.

"I'm sorry. Her body is as stiff as a board. A body this warm and early, you shouldn't see any signs of rigor mortis, unless she was paralyzed, but you said you saw her walk about?"

Lorenzo spoke up to this question. "I saw her clutching at herself, like she couldn't breathe, but she was able to walk."

"Well, there are no physical marks from which I could tell, so I would have to say she died from a stroke. I have to give the more definitive answer after the autopsy."

Melissa couldn't believe it because she was of the same age as the victim. "A stroke, at twenty-five? Doctor, I find that hard to believe. Look at her, she was so young, healthy and beautiful."

"Yes, it is possible, not common, but possible. I have seen where people that age are starting to get cancer."

Alan interjected, "Well, I can answer that for you, doctor. That is from all the high-fructose corn syrup they are putting into our food."

Dr. Ordonez responded, "You know you make a valid point, and when I have time I would like to research that theory more."

"See, Lorenzo, even the good doctor agrees with me," as Lorenzo rolls her eyes.

"Now, I didn't say I agreed, I just said that you have a valid argument. So is that what you think happen to this girl?"

"Honestly, I don't know. I like the facts before I make my conclusions."

Lorenzo interjected, "He not even on this case, he's just helping me on those two murders."

"Oh yeah! I heard you were able to deduce those as murders right away. Nice job! I was going to tell Sergeant Lorenzo anyway. She can be very stubborn sometimes," Ordonez said with a huge grin on his face.

Alan, acting like a kid at a baseball game, said, "I also want to say it is a privilege working with you, Dr. Ordonez. I will always remember the lecture you gave at my college. The lecture was about how to determine the time of death and its importance in an investigation."

"Thank you, I didn't know you brought a fan with you, Lorenzo."

"Okay, thank you, Dr. Ordonez. I look forward to your report in the morning. Bye now. Have a good night." Lorenzo was trying to dismiss the doctor the best she could. "I say we call it a night. Alan, get some rest. I have confidence you will think of a new lead before tomorrow morning. Meet me back in my office at 9:00 a.m."

As Melissa drove Alan back home, Alan was feeling somewhat uneasy. He wasn't sure what to do other than to go back and confront Dr. Leyland some more, which he knew Lorenzo would not approve of.

"Melissa."

"Yes, Alan."

"I have the uneasy feeling that we are going to lose this case and Lorenzo is going to hang the congressman for the murder. She will turn around and rub it back in my face."

"Oh, Alan, never doubt yourself. I know you can do it. I have all the confidence in you. You always come through. You will figure it out. I will tell you what I will do. When we get home, take a hot shower. I'll get some Bach playing in the bedroom. Bach makes you think more clearly, and I will give you a massage. You can't refuse that offer."

"You're right, I can't refuse such an offer. Okay, Melissa, I am in your capable hands.

CHAPTER 19

Before Alan was awakened by his alarm clock, which he had set for at 6:00 a.m., his phone rang. It was Sergeant Lorenzo. "Sorry to wake you Alan, but Dr. Ordonez has something to show all of us."

"What is it?" asked Alan, who was quite groggy.

"I don't know. I am actually on my way there. Dr. Ordonez said it was something confidential and something he had to show us all at once."

"Okay, we will be on our way."

Melissa, awakened by the commotion, asked what was going on.

"Melissa, Dr. Ordonez has something big for us. We've got to go now."

"Okay, give some time to get ready. I can't jet off like you can." Melissa was self-conscious about how she appeared in public at all times, no matter what the occasion.

A half hour later, Alan was waiting on Melissa, "Are you ready, Melissa?"

"Okay, Alan. Wait, what music are we playing in the car?"

"I am feeling a little counterculture, let's listen to Jefferson Airplane."

As "White Rabbit" was playing in Alan's Firebird, the sun had just risen in the east. Alan had to fight a huge sun glare as he hauled it on Interstate 94. That was not the only problem Alan had to fight with down the freeway. A red Dodge Viper was following Alan down the freeway. Alan spotted it as he drove past Ann Arbor. "Melissa," Alan said, "at the risk of sounding paranoid, I think that Dodge Viper has been on our ass since we left Jackson."

Melissa responded, "Well, what are you going to do?"

"I've got to try and lose it."

Just then, the passenger inside the red Dodge Viper fired a gun at Alan and Melissa. Melissa screamed as she heard the sound and she could feel the bullet whiz by their car.

"Hang on, Melissa. How does your favorite song go?"

Just as Alan said that, he shifted into high gear, revved the engine, and floored the Pontiac Firebird. He ran his speed machine as fast as it could go, easily driving over 110 miles per hour. Alan, with great skill, had the amazing ability to weave in and out of traffic. To no avail, the red Dodge Viper kept pace with Alan's Firebird.

"Alan," Melissa said, "you can't outrun that Viper."

"I know, Melissa. I am hoping someone on highway patrol is out and they will intervene in the chase. They are out every day. We can finally give them some real work to do."

Five more miles down the road and still no highway patrol to help out when Melissa said, "Alan, it's probably too early in the morning they would be beginning their shift, we can't run like this forever. Pretty soon we are going to hit the morning rush hour in Detroit."

"All right then, if we can't get highway patrol to help us out, maybe we can get Homeland Security."

"What are you talking about, Alan?"

"Let's go for a drive on the Metro Airport runway."

"Alan?"

"Here, Melissa, take my cell phone and call Sergeant Lorenzo and tell her to bring all the backup she can get."

"Do you know her number?" Melissa asked as if neither of them would have a clue.

"313-555-5046."

Melissa dialed the number, and Sergeant Lorenzo was on the other line. "Hello, Sergeant. This is Melissa Henneman."

"Where's Alan? Tell him I want him right now."

"Yes, well, we are in some trouble. These guys are chasing down I-94, and Alan can't get them off. Please come, they're shooting at us!"

"All right, just hold tight. Where are you at?"

"Alan is going to lead them to Metro Airport."

"Okay, we'll be right there."

When Melissa put Alan's cell phone on the armrest, she turned to Alan and asked, "How did you know Lorenzo's phone number?"

Alan answered, "Remember, she called my cell when we were in Fort Wayne with Kayla Gagne, and with my photographic memory . . ."

Melissa just shook her head in amazement. Alan never fails to amaze her. The task now was never like they had ever faced before. The pair had never had their life threatened before. Melissa was unsure if either was going to come out of this chase alive or at the least, badly hurt.

Ten miles later and no sign of the highway patrol chasing down after Alan and the red Dodge Viper, Alan continued to dodge traffic, sometimes even driving on the shoulder to avoid hitting a car. Alan got off on exit 198, heading for the Detroit Metro Airport.

Alan, never having done anything like this, was thinking about what he should do when he entered the airport. Alan thought if he went into the blue parking lot, which is the area the cars normally go to, the red Dodge Viper would have an easier chance to pin him down in a corner. Alan thought he stood a better chance in the open and drag race with the Viper on the runway. Alan saw a clearing to his right and made a bold move and drove right through it. Alan slashed across the grass, soaring at a very high rate of speed. Alan, even at one point, hit a bump on the ground that sent the black Firebird far above the ground. Alan then proceeded through a red, white, and blue hangar garage. The garage said "FLY SPIRIT" at the top of the building structure. One of the mechanics was inside and hurled himself across to avoid the speeding Firebird.

The mechanic pulled out his communication device and alerted security to, "a maniac in a black Trans Am. It could be Al-Qaeda. Get security out here now. This is an emergency."

The mechanic thought he had seen his life flash before eyes, but before he could collect his wits about him, he noticed out of the corner of his eye a red sports car coming right at him. It would have seemed like slow motion to him, but the mechanic flung himself toward the wall of the garage, just missing the brutal impact.

This was the time in the day where some of the early morning flights out of Detroit were warming their engines and getting ready for takeoff. Alan drove his black Trans Am onto the runway and daring the red Viper that was on him to follow him underneath the wings of the planes that were on the runway trying to takeoff. The pilots that were in the cockpits of the Delta and Northwest planes that were trying to takeoff were getting nervous and they just held their position. The pilots alerted the passengers that there would be a slight delay before takeoff but did not want to scare them in saying the reason why. They basically told passengers to remain calm.

Shortly after all the pilots made the announcement about the takeoff delay, a swarm of police and flashing lights were barreling down one of the runways. Most of these were TSA and Homeland Security personnel. Lorenzo's crew was coming from the north end of the airfield. Alan and his pursuer were drag racing on the runway, splitting the airfield down the middle.

Some of the passengers aboard Northwest flight finally saw cars racing each other on one of the runways. A passenger shouted out, "Hey this looks like a scene from *Smokey and the Bandit*!"

All of the passengers went to the left side windows to look at the action taking place. The passengers aboard the plane were quickly admonished for leaving their seats. They were ordered back to remain in their seats until further instructions were announced.

The gunman in the Dodge Viper was starting to fire more bullets at Alan's Firebird. They got to the point where they were almost side by side, when Alan did a stunning move: slamming on the brakes, shifting into reverse, driving the car backward, then spinning the car 180 degrees to head back to where all the disco lights were at. All of the cars converged into one spot, except for the red Viper. He drove off, cut through some grass, rammed through a thin wire fence, and then got back on the freeway, almost wrecking a few cars in the process. The Viper however was not in its pristine condition. The fence did some damage that was easily noticeable. Alan and Melissa got out of the car. Homeland Security beat Lorenzo's crew and got to Alan and Melissa first.

"Down on the ground, now!"

Alan and Melissa did what they said. Homeland Security was dressed in all black with full riot gear on, looking like they were getting ready for a war. Two of these black dressed men went over to Alan and Melissa and proceeded to tie their hands up.

Alan spoke up, "Look, Sergeant Lorenzo will be here to explain everything."

"SHUT UP! You don't say a word until we ask you something," one of the black-dressed men screamed into Alan's ear.

Just then, Lorenzo's crew arrived with her posse. "Out of the way, I am in charge of this."

The black-dressed man who just yelled at Alan looked over, not taking kindly to having authority defied. "Who the hell are you?"

"Sergeant Lorenzo, Detroit Homicide."

"Homicide? There is no homicide here. I don't know who called you, but this is a matter of Homeland Security, we don't need you, so go back."

"This *is* a part of my homicide investigation. These two that you have on the ground are working for me. They are the ones who called me and said they were being shot at."

The black-dressed man looked confused as could be was not willing to believe Lorenzo's take so easily. He still has his M16 rifle pointed at Alan, and Alan had remained perfectly still the whole time. The black-dressed man was looking for any reason he could justify beating Alan. Lorenzo kept insisting that they were with her.

"This isn't standard operating procedure. I am going to have to call my supervisor."

"Look, I am Detroit Police. You have my word. We are all on the same team."

"I still have to call this in."

"Fine, do what you have to do, but can I talk with my partners?"

"Okay, but I am going to have my partner listen, because they are suspects in a terrorism plot."

"Terrorism plot, my ass! I just told you they are with me and we are working a murder investigation."

"All the same, ma'am, I still have to insist."

The mechanic, who was nearly run over twice in the Fly Spirit garage, ran through the middle of all the Homeland Security and TSA personnel, yelling, "Al-Qaeda, Al-Qaeda!" One of the black-dressed man's assistants was ordered to chase him down to ask him his accounts of the events.

Alan and Melissa slowly got up, brushed themselves off, and talked with Lorenzo. Alan said to Lorenzo, "Hey, Lorenzo, who is the conspiracy theorist now?"

"This is ridiculous. Just because he works at the federal level doesn't mean he can push people like me who are at the municipal level."

"Well, Lorenzo, this is what I was warning you about in our Homeland Security class, the rising police state."

"Are you both all right?"

"Yeah, but I would feel a lot better if we could get away from these jackals."

A black-dressed man got off the phone just to ask Alan and Melissa their names.

"Thanks for being here, I owe you one," said Alan.

"No, thanks to you we got our first real break in the case."

"Yes, apparently one of the rocks we turned over was the correct one, and the people didn't like what we uncovered. How much you want a bet is was Dr. Leyland? He seemed the most pissed off."

"Okay, you have a valid point—" In midsentence, Lorenzo was interrupted by the black-dressed man, "All right, my supervisor says these two have to come with us for interrogation."

Lorenzo could not believe was she was hearing. "This is ridiculous."

"Sergeant, these two, their names are on a list of suspicious terrorist activity. They have libertarian political points of view."

Lorenzo said, "I know his politics are weird, but what does that have to do with anything?"

Alan spoke up because he just knew what this about. "I know what this is about—"

"You SHUT UP!" screamed the black-dressed man.

Alan, refusing to obey the order, said, "The MIAC report."

When Alan said that, the black-dressed man struck a blow and belted Alan in the mouth.

Lorenzo, not pleased with the behavior of the black-dressed man, asked him, "What is the MIAC report?" The black-dressed man, with hesitancy, answered the sergeant's question.

"The Missouri Information Analysis Center, MIAC for short, provides officers an organization of public safety, which includes local, state, and federal agencies, as well as the public and private divisions that will collect, evaluate, analyze, and disseminate information and intelligence to the agencies tasked with Homeland Security responsibilities in a timely, effective, and secure manner. Have you not been getting our memos, Sergeant? Everything is on our Web site, www.miacx.org."

"No, I haven't. You see, I have been too busy fighting crime. If you haven't noticed, Detroit is a crime-ridden city. For instance, as I have told you, these two are helping me with a murder investigation."

"Maybe you wouldn't have to work so hard if you employed some of the strategies that the MIAC uses. The MIAC is a tool to collect incident reports of suspicious activities to be evaluated and analyzed in an effort to identify potential trends or patterns of terrorist or criminal operations within the state of Missouri. The same model you can use here in Michigan, if you wanted to. MIAC also works as a vehicle for two-way communication between federal, state, and local law enforcement community within our region."

The black-dressed man continued, "See we are about communication and keeping the channels of communication open within all departments. We can't let another 9/11 happen. MIAC is just part of the federal 'fusion' effort now underway around the country. As of 2009, there were fifty-eight fusion centers around the country, and we plan to have thousands more professionals deployed in the years to come. The Department of Homeland Security has provided more than $254 million from FY 2004-2007 to state and local governments to support the centers. Missouri is a participant in this federal intelligence effort."

Sergeant Lorenzo responded, "That all sounds nice, but what does this have to do with libertarians?"

The black-dressed man answered, "We're just keeping tabs on them because we think they might be terrorists."

"You think they might be? That's thin, sir, you must have evidence to justify what you are doing."

According to the report, MIAC claims that there are members that are of a "right-wing" militia movement continuously exploiting world events in order to increase their participation. Due to the current economical and political climate, a fertile environment for militia activity has been created to be exploited by constitutionalists, white supremacists, and libertarians, the latter usually use demonizing activists as dangerous and potentially violent lunatics."

Sergeant Lorenzo was confused now. "Wait, this was never brought out during the 9/11 investigation or written in the 9/11 commission report. The kind of jihad that you're referring to was said to be from an extreme fundamentalist Islam religion. How do you account for that?" The black-dressed man did not have an answer. "Look, sir, whatever your name is, I don't know who is crazier, you or my libertarian associate here, but I need to go on with my investigation."

As Lorenzo was starting to leave with Alan and Melissa, the black-dressed man said, "All right, Sergeant, you can go and take your assistants with you, but I am warning you, be careful who your friends are and which ones you can trust."

Lorenzo gave a shout back, "Yeah, I'll remember that."

CHAPTER 20

Lorenzo told Alan and Melissa to follow her. She promised them they would have the escort of her colleagues. They all arrived at the station and proceeded to see Dr. Ordonez who had been waiting patiently to show them the victim Tiffany Burton. It was 11:00 a.m. now, and Dr. Ordonez was wondering what had happened to everyone. His wonderment would finally come to an end when he heard the voices of Lorenzo and Alan from up above coming down the stairs. Dr. Ordonez could hear the excitement and the commotion of the murder attempt of Alan and Melissa. Lorenzo swung the glass door of Dr. Ordonez's morgue wide-open. "Sorry to make you wait, doctor, we have had an interesting morning."

"So I hear, but that's okay, because I have more to show you. See, while you were gone, I was able to do more for our victim and I got a preliminary toxic report, which you are going to find interesting."

"Very good, but before you begin, I have to ask Alan a question. How do you know about any MIAC report? From the sound of talking to that black-dressed man, no civilian is supposed to know about it?"

"Lorenzo, you should know by now, I am more informed than your average citizen. I don't make up any of the information I tell people. It's really no secret, you know."

"How is that?"

"The black-dressed man admitted to you it's out in the open for the public to see. It is on the Internet. They have their own Web site. Of course, knowing what to look for is entirely a different matter. Anyone can find out about what is really going on this world, but the public is not going to."

"Why not?"

"Because they are lazy and too materialistic, and what I mean by that is they are more worried about their pocketbook, you know how much money they have, possessions, baubles, their love life, the deadlines they have got to meet at work, how their favorite sports team is doing. There are a million distractions that keep them from finding out the truth.

"The truth about what, the conspiracy that is unfolding? In your dreams, Alan Williams."

"I like to think of them as the mysteries of this life on this planet, but call it what you like, I am know that I am right."

"Well, since you are so sure, did everything that the black-dressed man told us about the MIAC report, is it the truth?"

"It is truthful in a sense, this is the official claim that Homeland Security makes on their Web site, but there were some details that he left out."

"Okay, Alan, tell us. Tell us what you only know and nobody in this department knows about a classified Homeland Security report."

"I would be happy to tell you. The MIAC report is similar to one created by the Phoenix Federal Bureau of Investigation and the Joint Terrorism Task Force. You remember teaching this to us in our Homeland Security class."

Lorenzo acknowledged Alan. "JTTFs have been very successful. It resulted in the arrest of fifteen terrorists of the 1993 World Trade Center bombing."

"That's my point, Lorenzo. There was nothing wrong with our policies before 9/11. Now the document that I am talking about came as result of 9/11, and it explicitly designates 'defenders' of the Constitution as 'right-wing extremists.' The MIAC report expands significantly on that earlier document. In order to synthetically intensify the perceived threat of terrorism, MIAC rolls in Christian Identity, white nationalism, 'militant' antiabortion activists, opposition to illegal immigration, and income tax resistance as red alerts or the new warning signs of homegrown terrorism. MIAC deliberately distorts the lines between distinct political ideologies and overemphasizes the possibility for violence in a rundown of the organizational makeup of the militia movement and a section describing how these people try to train in 'combat readiness.' According to the MIAC report, those who oppose a world government or the idea of a New World Order, NAFTA, federalization of the states, and gun control are a threat to the police."

"Whoa, stop, Alan! Are you saying that the terrorists are people who believe in a New World Order?"

"No, what I am saying is that the MIAC report places all US citizens in the crosshairs as being as potential terrorists. We have seen this before in our history. The Red Scare and the Palmer Raids occurred in 1920. At this time, World War I had ended, bringing the United States into a war on Communism. Now today, the news media will say the war on terrorism.

Aren't those two phrases similar? They are just catchy phrases that rally the citizenry up so that they will go along with what the government is doing. Newspapers openly attacked Communists because they spoke out against the United States involvement in World War I. The Communists were regarded as evil, so evil they simply had to go away at all cost. For who would dare speak out against the war, even when the right was granted under the First Amendment.

"Among the most notorious anti-Communist figures was Alexander Palmer, US attorney general under Woodrow Wilson. Palmer conducted raids on those suspected to be on the left side of the political spectrum. These included anarchists and Communists. Anyone in possession of items deemed inappropriate would be subject to penalty, including deportation. This would, in effect, make them go away.

"Now this is what is happening today. The people who view the military, National Guard, and law enforcement as a force that will confiscate their firearms and place them in FEMA concentration camps, they are the new Communists. The document even says they are in a section titled 'You are the Enemy.' The MIAC is attempting to radicalize the police against political activity guaranteed by the U.S. Constitution and the Bill of Rights."

Sergeant Lorenzo and Dr. Ordonez were just floored by what Alan had to say. Lorenzo said, "I have got to hand it to you, Alan. Despite what I think of your perspective, you defend your points very well." A moment later, a thought crept into the mind of Lorenzo. "So I view myself more of a conservative political ideology and I strongly oppose abortion, would that make me an enemy of this MIAC report?"

Alan answered, "Yes, it would. Now understand something, they don't put that in, because the government hates antiabortionists. Abortion and terrorism have no correlation with one another. They just wanted to lump everybody into one, so that it would be impossible not to be considered a terrorist. Now do you see why it is impossible to sacrifice liberty for security, it can't be done? I mean, we give up our rights and freedoms, it may prevent a crime, but we will never be secure with ourselves, we will think everybody's a terrorist!"

"Well, Alan, that is an intellectual debate we can have some other time. Right now, Dr. Ordonez has got something quite interesting, as it relates to our murder investigation and he has been waiting extremely patiently. Doctor, proceed."

Everybody in the morgue fixated on the corpse of Tiffany Burton. Her lifeless body lay on the silver slab. You could see a whitening of the skin—the first signs of rigor mortis.

"Thanks, Lorenzo. I initially ruled this woman's death as a stroke. Then I was starting the routine preliminaries on the autopsy and I noticed a puncture wound on the inside of her left arm."

"She was stabbed?" Lorenzo questioned.

"No, it is from a syringe."

Lorenzo remembered and said, "Her friends did say that they went and picked her up from Walgreen's in Ann Arbor at four thirty, which was approximately a half hour before her death. She went there for a flu shot."

"Well, that fits, because of this letter I got from a neurologist friend of mine."

Alan was intrigued and said, "What does the letter say?"

"It is a confidential letter that went to all senior neurologists from the government. It warns that a new H1N1 vaccine is linked to a deadly nerve disease. The deadly nerve disease is called Guillain-Barre syndrome."

"You think that was this girl died of?" asked Lorenzo.

"Yes, without a doubt. Guillain-Barre syndrome attacks the lining of the nerves. You can tell by her arms and her legs that nerves are shot and out of whack."

"Would this Guillain-Barre syndrome cause her paralysis and difficulty in breathing?"

"Absolutely," Dr. Ordonez said confidently.

Alan asked Dr. Ordonez the next question. "If the vaccine is what triggers Guillain-Barre syndrome, what is in the vaccine that causes it to do that, and why do they let it be distributed if it is not safe?"

"Well, I can't answer the second question, but the first question I am happy you brought up because that is what is so interesting and the reason I called all of you in here. I did some research and got an ingredients list from the Center for Disease Control on the new H1N1 vaccine. The same ingredients that were found in the toxicology of Mark Lewis and Casey Thomas are the same ingredients found in the new H1N1 vaccine. The formaldehyde, thimerosal, caustic soda, and even the sheep's blood were all in there. I bet when we get full toxicology back from Ms. Burton here, we will find all the same things."

Lorenzo said, "They were all vaccinated."

Alan said, "Designed as a soft-kill weapon, but why kill them now? Lorenzo, we got to go back and question Dr. Leyland. He is our man, I know it. Remember, when we were all in his office, what was the first thing we heard him say?"

Melissa tried to answer, "I am Dr. Leyland?"

"No, it was before he even saw us and he was helping that corpulent woman out the door, he said, "Don't forget to call us on Saturday to confirm your scheduled flu shot."

Melissa finally remembered and exclaimed, "Yes, he did say that!"

"Look, I can question him later, but I can't bring you two along with me because he will sue us for police harassment," explained Lorenzo.

Alan tried to compromise. "Can't you get wired up, at least so we talk to you and we can hear what is going on."

"Okay, but I am going to have a couple boys from traffic to sit and watch you while I go inside. I will handcuff the two of you if I have to."

"Sounds kinky," Melissa said.

"Dr. Ordonez," Lorenzo said it as if she was getting sickened by all of the day's conspiracy theories said, "is there anything else that is in that letter that I should know about?"

"The letter refers to when there was swine flu panic in 1976. It said that more people died from the vaccination than they did from actual flu itself in 1976. There were five hundred cases of Guillain-Barre syndrome, all as a result of the vaccine. The vaccine may have increased the risk of contracting Guillain-Barre syndrome by eight times. The vaccine was withdrawn after just ten weeks when the link with Guillain-Barre syndrome and the vaccine became clear. The US government was forced to pay out millions of dollars to those affected."

"If they knew this about what happened in 1976, what makes the government think they will be successful now?"

"They have said that the vaccine is new and it is a slightly different strain than the one in 1976. The concern does remain for the risk of Guillain-Barre syndrome. My friend told me that he would not have the swine flu vaccine."

"Thank you, doctor."

CHAPTER 21

As a couple of officers were wiring up Lorenzo before she was going to interview Dr. Leyland, Alan and Melissa were in the backseat of the police van. Melissa said to Alan, "You tried to tell them it was Dr. Leyland, and they didn't listen to you."

"I know."

"Why do we have to talk to him? Why can't they arrest him?"

"We don't have enough proof. We have to have probable cause to make an arrest."

"But you know he did it."

"Yes, but knowing and proving are two different things. We know and can prove that all the victims were vaccinated, but we can't prove that Dr. Leyland is responsible for them getting the vaccine. Furthermore, Lewis didn't die of the vaccine, he died due to strangulation, remember?"

"Well, how do we prove that Dr. Leyland killed those people?"

"I don't know. I'm working on it."

Lorenzo finally got ready to go in and conduct the interview with Dr. Leyland.

"Humor me, Sergeant, and take this pen with you."

"Why do I need a pen? I'm not going to sign anything."

"Just take the pen and wear in your front pocket."

Lorenzo accepted the pen and placed it in her front pocket.

"Now, remember stay in the van or else. Boys, make sure they don't go anywhere under any circumstances."

Lorenzo went in to the doctor's office. Lorenzo asked if the doctor could see her, and the receptionist said it would all right, but it may take ten minutes because the doctor was busy. Lorenzo said she would wait. The ten minutes felt more like twenty when Dr. Leyland finally walked out to the lobby to greet Lorenzo.

"Sergeant Lorenzo, what brings you back again? This isn't another formal apology? I hope this isn't more about the Lewis murder?"

"Uh, yes, I am here in the inquiry of his death, but I am coming to you more for your profession medical advice."

"Oh really, your assistant not lurking with you today, is he?"

"No, sir, don't worry, he was rebuked, scolded, and chided for his tirade."

"Well, what can I do for you?"

"We found traces of formaldehyde, thimerosal, caustic soda, and sheep's blood in toxicology reports in all our victims."

"Victims? I thought you were just investigating the one death of Mark Lewis?"

"We are. But since then, we have had a couple more homicides. One, we believe, was due to natural causes. What would something that would have those toxic ingredients in them?"

"I wouldn't know."

"What about flu vaccines?"

"No, vaccines wouldn't have thimerosol in them. Thimerosal is a derivative of mercury. The weight of the mercury inside would have serious adverse effects that we would be seeing the results of it. I have been a doctor for forty years. We tell people to get the MMR shot ever since I have been in this profession, and there is no mercury in any of the vaccines. That is just a crazy conspiracy theory."

"What is MMR?"

"MMR stands for measles, mumps, and rubella. It is the shot you have to get before you start school."

"How safe do you think a vaccine is?"

"Look, no vaccine could ever be 100 percent safe truly. I think that is impossible. The Center of Disease and Control is placed with the task of assuring the safety of the vaccine, and I assure you, they are very good at what they do. As a check and balance, there is oversight by the Food and Drug Administration. They conduct trials and postlicensure monitoring."

"What causes Guillain-Barre syndrome?"

"Guillain-Barre syndrome? How are you getting this? I thought Mark Lewis was strangled?"

"Please, just answer the question."

"Guillain-Barre syndrome is a rare disorder in which your body's immune system attacks your nerves. Frailty and numbness in your hands and feet are usually the first symptoms. These feelings and sensations can rapidly spread, eventually paralyzing your whole body."

"What is the cause of this rare disorder?"

"The cause is unknown, but usually it involves an infection of the lungs or the digestive tract."

"A vaccine couldn't cause Guillain-Barre syndrome?"

"I don't know, I never heard of such a case. I don't understand what does this have to do with the murder?"

"It may be nothing, but we have to check out all angles of the case. Thank you for the information, doctor."

Lorenzo walked out of the doctor's office and met up with her team a couple of miles away. Lorenzo echoed back to Alan and Melissa what Dr. Leyland had to say on the vaccine and Guillain-Barre syndrome.

"He's lying, I'm telling you."

"Okay, Alan, but how are we going to prove it?"

"Why don't we go to Walgreens and ask the pharmacist for an insert of the H1N1 flu vaccine?"

"An insert?"

"Yeah, the information sheet that lists the indications for its use, dosage, side effects, etc., and what ingredients are inside it. Yeah, now we will see who is telling the truth."

"All right, take us to Walgreens. Can I have my pen back?"

"What? Oh, yeah sure. Here you go. Why did you have me carry that inside?" Lorenzo asked as one of officers got the van started and commenced to the nearest Walgreens.

"This pen is no ordinary pen. It has a hidden camera inside, and it recorded your interview with Dr. Leyland."

Sergeant Lorenzo raised her voice as if she couldn't be trusted. "You didn't trust me, did you?"

"No, that's not it at all. I wanted to see if I could pick up any clues about the good doctor. This pen comes apart and has a USB drive inside it. When we are done at Walgreens, I would like to borrow you computer, Lorenzo, and see what it picked up."

CHAPTER 22

A few minutes later, a police van showed up in the parking lot of a Walgreens pharmacy. Lorenzo, Alan, and Melissa walked up to the pharmacy desk and asked for the pharmacist. Lorenzo flashed her badge and asked for the insert to the H1N1 flu vaccine.

"We are investigating a homicide and we know the victim was vaccinated before her death, we think there may be a connection."

The pharmacist, taken aback by the request, went in the back to try and find what was being requested.

"I am sorry, we don't have an insert to the Flu Mist, but we have the insert for the injection vaccine made by Novartis."

"That will work."

Alan took the fact sheet with him back to the van. Alan opened it up and read the information aloud to Lorenzo. This is what was in the fact sheet:

> INDICATIONS AND USAGE
> Influenza A (H1N1) 2009 Monovalent Vaccine is an inactivated influenza virus vaccine indicated for active immunization of persons 4 years of age and older against influenza disease caused by pandemic (H1N1) 2009 virus (1).

"Pandemic, my ass! More people died from the regular flu than they did swine flu!"

Lorenzo was curious and had to ask, "How do you know, Alan?"

Alan spouted out figures that made Lorenzo's head spin. "Slightly over eleven thousand people died from the swine flu. On average, thirty-six thousand die from regular flu and that comes from the Center for Disease and Control."

"Again, how do you know this?"

Melissa responded, "Remember, photographic memory."

As the police van was making their way back to Lorenzo's office, Alan continued to read the insert.

> DOSAGE FORMS AND STRENGTH
>
> Influenza A (H1N1) 2009 Monovalent Vaccine, a sterile suspension for intramuscular injection, is supplied in two presentations:
>
> Prefilled single dose syringe, 0.5-mL. Thimerosal, a mercury derivative used during manufacture, is removed by subsequent purification steps to a trace amount (less than or equal to 1 mcg mercury per 0.5-mL dose) (3, 11)
>
> Multidose vial, 5-mL. Contains thimerosal, a mercury derivative (25 mcg mercury per 0.5-mL dose). Thimerosal is added as preservative. (3, 11)
>
> WARNINGS AND PRECAUTIONS
>
> If Guillain-Barre Syndrome has occurred within 6 weeks of receipt of prior influenza vaccine, the decision to give influenza A (H1N1) 2009 Monovalent Vaccine should be based on careful consideration of the potential benefits and risks. (5.1)
>
> Immunocompromised persons may have a reduced immune response to Influenza A (H1N1) 2009 Monovalent Vaccine (5.2)

After hearing what was in the insert, Lorenzo has to accept that they have been putting mercury in the vaccines and that it is possible to get Guillain-Barre syndrome.

"See, I told you Dr. Leyland was lying through his teeth."

"You know, Alan I never saw you as the I-told-you-so type. It still doesn't answer as to why the doctor would lie about this."

"He expected you to believe him as matter-of-fact and never to be questioned. He counted on that, and you might have had I not been here."

Just then, a thought occurred to Melissa. "Alan, what does it mean when it says that im . . . muno . . . compromised persons may have a reduced immune response?"

"It means that the vaccine weakens a person's immune system. If the body's immune system has been weakened to the point where the body had no immunity left, withered through other vaccinations or drugs, the body will not be able to handle this vaccination. Perhaps it is the reason why it is possible to get Guillain-Barre syndrome. Bear in mind this is speculation on my part, I am not a doctor. For the longest time, I have never been able to trust doctors."

"You got a conspiracy theory about doctors?" questioned Lorenzo, not sure if she could stomach another one.

"No, it is just of my opinion that doctors only push for two things, drugs and surgery. I believe to stay healthy they should push vitamins and strengthening the body's immune system."

Alan turned the fact sheet over, as there was another side to the insert. Alan read silently and then found something quite intriguing.

"Hey guys, check this out! Dr. Ordonez will find this very interesting."

"What is it?"

> **6.4 Other Adverse Reactions Associated with Influenza Vaccination**
>
> The 1976 swine influenza vaccine was associated with an increased frequency of Guillain-Barre Syndrome. Evidence for a casual relation of Guillain-Barre Syndrome with subsequent vaccines prepared from other influenza viruses is unclear. If influenza vaccine does pose a risk, it is probably slightly more than 1 additional case/1 million persons vaccinated. Neurological disorders temporally associated with influenza vaccination such as encephalopathy, optic neuritis/neuropathy, partial facial paralysis, and brachial plexus neuropathy have been reported. Microscopic polyangiitis (vasculitis) has been reported temporally associated with influenza vaccinations

"Wonderful," cried Melissa.

"Well, Lorenzo, I think it is safe to say that Tiffany Burton died from Guillain-Barre syndrome as result of getting the swine flu vaccination."

"Yes, but what I don't understand is why the government keeps trying these vaccines. It sounds like they do more damage than they are said to prevent. The bigger question is how this explains why Mark Lewis was strangled. Where do the Freemasons and Bohemian Grove fit into all this? Is Dr. Leyland our man?"

"Good questions all, Lorenzo. Let's go find out the answers."

They arrived at the Detroit Police Station, and Alan could not wait to use Lorenzo's computer. Alan desperately was hoping a small clue would pop up for them. Alan inserted the USB drive into the USB port in the back of Lorenzo's computer. Video footage immediately came up of Lorenzo walking into the doctor's office. The interview went just as Lorenzo told Alan and Melissa. The video exposed and caught the lies Dr. Leyland was saying about vaccines and Guillain-Barre syndrome. In the middle of the video, Alan noticed something metallic on the blue tie that Dr. Leyland was wearing. The metallic object looked to be about a couple of centimeters in diameter.

"What is that on his tie?"

"I can't tell."

"Lorenzo, you got something that we can pause this and blow that thing up?"

"Yes, let me back on my computer. I think I am a little more tech savvy than you."

Lorenzo was able to do what Alan requested, and what Alan saw turned his eyes wide-open. Dr. Leyland was wearing the symbol of Freemasonry.

"There you have it, Lorenzo. Dr. Leyland is a Freemason. He's got the inverted square and compass with the capital G in the middle. No doubt about it. What do you think, Lorenzo? Do we have enough probable cause to make an arrest? We at least got enough to properly interrogate him this time?"

"Okay, Alan, I will fill out the affidavit and see if the magistrate will sign it, but it may be a problem."

"Why is that, Lorenzo?"

"The magistrate is a Freemason."

CHAPTER 23

Lorenzo came back to Alan with a signed affidavit allowing Dr. Leyland to be brought in for questioning. "You got the warrant, excellent," exclaimed Alan.

"Yes, but lucky for you that Judge Whitaker owed me a favor. He wasn't too happy about signing off on this, but I proved to him that I had established probable cause. You see, Alan, I know the rules. I play by them."

"Well, if nothing is stopping us, let's go."

It was a good thirty minutes before Alan and Lorenzo arrived at the residence of Dr. John Leyland. On the way, Lorenzo decided to pick Alan's brain just for the fun of it.

"Alan," said Lorenzo, "You are one unique individual. What makes you tick? How did you become so conspiratorial? It makes for a lousy social life, but you seem to do fine with Melissa. It also makes for a pretty good detective, I have noticed. You have the instincts of a hound. Where did you develop senses like that?"

Alan responded, "When I was a kid, I confess I isolated myself from the world. Instead of playing with the other kids, I sat inside watching television. I watched Sherlock Holmes mysteries, game shows, and my favorite, the *X-Files*."

"Ah, now it is starting to make sense. You have an extreme introverted personality."

"Yes, while I appreciate the knowledge I have gained through my dreamy vegetation state of unconsciousness, I would recommend that I would not have bombarded my brain with sensory images the television can damage you."

"What are you talking about?"

"It doesn't matter what your diet and exercise is like, but TV will increase your risk of dying from heart disease. This is according to a recent report in

Circulation: Journal of the American Heart Association. The study conducted in Australia said that '8,800 adult men and women for an average of six years and found that every hour spent in front of the TV translated into an 11 percent increase in the risk of death from any cause, a 9 percent increase in the risk of death from cancer and an 18 percent increase in the risk of death from cardiovascular disease.'

"I think you worry about some of the little things too much. You should live life a little. Okay, we're here. I will go in and handle this. You just stay back and give me space."

"Yes, Lorenzo. I wouldn't dream of interfering in your investigation, especially not now."

Lorenzo knocked on the door, which was white, to a house otherwise built entirely out of bricks. Dr. Leyland answered and was stunned to see Sergeant Lorenzo again.

"Dr. Leyland."

"Yes, we meet again. What can I do for you this time?" Dr. Leyland caught a glance and saw Alan in the car waiting. "What! Why is he hanging around here? I thought I warned you to keep him out of my hair."

"Yes, well, all bets are off now, because we have a warrant to take you downtown to ask you some more questions, which you seem to be unwilling to answer. You are not obliged to say anything at this time. Do you understand your rights?"

"Yes, I understand my bloody rights, and the first one is that I want my lawyer."

"Sir, I think that would be a good idea."

Dr. Leyland was taken into custody by Sergeant Lorenzo and rode back to the police station.

CHAPTER 24

When Lorenzo drove back to the station, she told Alan not to ask any questions because Dr. Leyland had already asked for the solicitation of legal counsel. Lorenzo did allow Alan observe the interrogation from behind the two-way mirror. Alan was ordered in the strictest sense not to enter the interrogation under any circumstances. Dr. Leyland's lawyer had arrived. The lawyer was Don Okoniewski. Okoniewski mainly went by the title of Mr. O. Mr. O was a big-time lawyer in Detroit. He had never lost a case in his life and was quickly making a name in the state of Michigan, let alone the city of Detroit. At age 28, which is roughly the same age as Alan Williams, some say that if Mr. O was old enough to pass the bar, he could have gotten Dr. Kevorkian out of prison. Mr. O was probably the last person Sergeant Lorenzo wanted to see. Dr. Leyland's attorney spoke first before Lorenzo could get a chance to say anything.

"I'll have you know that this arrest is absolutely outrageous and when we are done in here we are filing a harassment lawsuit. I have asked Dr. Leyland not to answer any of your questions."

"But you don't even know what I am about to ask."

"It doesn't matter. You are trying to pin this suicide/murder, you can't even get that straight, on Dr. Leyland, when my client is completely innocent."

"Oh, I don't know about that. Dr. Leyland, where did you get your medical degree?"

"Strike that," interrupted Mr. O. "Mark Lewis and Casey Thomas did not die from medical complications. This is not a case of malpractice. You have no right to ask these questions."

"Mr. O, please humor me. Let me show you what we have got. We got a girl on the slab because she died of Guillain-Barre syndrome as a result of a vaccination. When we asked Dr. Leyland for medical information into our murder of Mark Lewis, he said, and I quote, 'Vaccines wouldn't have thimerosol in them. The weight of the mercury inside would have serious adverse effects that we would be seeing the results of it.' You also said that there was no mercury in any of the vaccines and you also said that a vaccine could not cause Guillain-Barre syndrome. Well, we got this from the pharmacist at the local Walgreens."

Sergeant Lorenzo began to show Dr. Leyland the insert and point out where is says that the vaccine contains thimerosol and how it warns of Guillain-Barre syndrome. "So we have to ask, since you're a medical professional of forty years, how could you be so far wrong? In other words, why did you lie?"

Dr. Leyland looked at his attorney, waiting to see if Mr. O would let him answer the question. Mr. O nodded at him and acknowledged him to answer this question.

"Okay, I admit I lied to you about the mercury. I was paid by one of the top pharmaceutical companies $75,000 to distribute as many vaccinations as I could. The goal was to distribute about five billion. Big Pharma would have made billions in profits. The problem was that nobody was volunteering on their own to take them, despite the World Health Organization warning and efforts."

"Let me get this straight. You intentionally deceived the public about their health, gave an unsafe and untested vaccine simply for the money! What about you're Hippocratic oath to the health and well-being of your patients? The oath you swore that says 'I will neither give a deadly drug to anybody if asked for it, nor will I make a suggestion to this effect."

"That is the classic version. We don't use that oath anymore."

"Well, doctor, I think you need to go back to it."

Just then, a message was hand-delivered to Lorenzo by a fellow police officer. The message said that Lieutenant Patrick was back, and he wanted to see Lorenzo and Alan immediately in his office.

"Interview suspended at 3:07 p.m."

"Are you going to charge my client?"

"I haven't decided, but we got enough to hold him for twenty-four hours. I am not done questioning him yet, but there will ethics review and I am going to see to it that Dr. Leyland never practice medicine again."

Lorenzo left the room and told Alan that Lieutenant Patrick was here and he had news to share back from his infiltration of the freemason lodges.

"You know, Alan, after that interview you have me convinced that Dr. Leyland is our murderer, but I am still unsure as to his true motivation. I am going to walk in to Patrick's office and tell him." Lorenzo walked into Patrick's office and immediately said, "Lieutenant, I know who our murderer is."

"I know who it is too. It is State Representative Tony Kiebler."

CHAPTER 25

"Kiebler!" Lorenzo and Alan cried out in disbelief. "Lieutenant, I know you have been working a different angle on the investigation, but we found out that Dr. Leyland is a Freemason and we found a new girl dead in a bar with Guillain-Barre syndrome as a result of vaccination and we have—"

"Yes, I agree all the victims were vaccinated as a result from toxicology. They all had the formaldehyde and the mercury. Remember, our first two victims died as a result of laceration and a blow to the head. A vaccine would not have been able to do that so some other method was used in those cases. However, I found out which Masonic lodge Thomas went to. Thomas went to the Pyramid Lodge. It is not a very big lodge, so everybody pretty much knew everyone in the membership. Interestingly enough, Representative Kiebler is also a Freemason and attended this month's meeting. As being one the three contacts of Mark Lewis', he rose to the top of the suspect list. I also inquired if the lodge knew Dr. Leyland, and all of them said they do not see him at that lodge. Remember, Alan, it was you who said that our killer had to attend the same lodge as Casey Thomas."

Lorenzo rebutted, "Kiebler's secretary gave Mr. Kiebler his alibi and said he was in his office during the time of the murder."

Patrick responded, "Time to find out who is telling the truth."

Both Lorenzo and Patrick noticed Alan very quiet, which was unusual for him. "Alan, are you all right?"

"Has anybody seen Melissa? Where did she go?"

"We left her back here when we went to go pick up Dr. Leyland."

Just then, another sergeant went to Lorenzo with a report that the All Points Bulletin came back on the red Dodge Viper. It was driving erratically westbound on Hunt Street.

"That's just around the block from here!"

"They've got Melissa!" Alan yelped, and his heart felt like it jumped through his chest.

Lieutenant Patrick got on the public address system in the station. "Attention, attention, all available personnel, in pursuit a red Dodge Viper. The car was last seen on Hunt Street, and its fenders were smashed in. Alan, you wouldn't happen to have an idea where they are taking her?"

"Not exactly, but I can guess that they are taking her to a secret location."

"No time to talk, don't worry, Alan, we will find her. Let's GO!"

Alan ran as fast as he could to his car, thinking about how he was about to drive like Dale Earnhardt through the streets of Detroit. When he got to the '77 Pontiac Firebird, there was a manila envelope on the windshield. He opened the package and found a gold-plated iron railroad spike with the number 1851 engraved on the spike. The spike looked very old. Alan thought to himself that the kidnappers wanted him to have this as a clue. Instead of going on the wild-goose chase after the red Dodge Viper, Alan decided to follow up on the clue. The spike, as mysterious as it was, gave Alan a bit of assurance that the kidnappers would not harm Melissa until he followed up on the clue that was provided. Alan honestly did not have a clue where they could have taken Melissa, so he decided to head for the library and find out what he could about the mysterious railroad spike.

Alan did race through the streets of Detroit to get to the library. Alan had about fifteen minutes because the library was about to close for the day. Alan tried to calm himself and said there is a plenty of time, just get the information.

"I would like to see a reference librarian, please."

"Of course, there is one available over there, but be aware we only have fifteen minutes before the library closes."

"That is okay, I will take any time I can get."

The reference librarian, Mr. Fryman greeted Alan. "Sir, how can I help you?"

"This railroad spike was left on my car and it has significance to the case I am working on. I hope I could extract information as to where it might have come from."

"Sir, isn't this a job for forensics?"

"I don't have time to deal with forensics. Are you a local man?"

"Yes."

"What are some railroads around here?"

"There is a short line railroad here that began in 1998."

"No, I don't think that its, because you see here the number 1851 is engraved on the spike. I believe that stands for the year. Search for the railroads that were in existence in 1851 in Detroit."

"The only thing that came up was the Michigan Central Railroad, which still exists today. The only connection to 1851 was that it connected with the Joliet and Northern Indiana line. Is this what you are looking for?"

"No, I don't think they're heading for Joliet. There's got to be something that possesses a secret to it or maybe a conspiracy. I am looking for a secret location that ties it to 1851. Put something along those lines into the search engine and see what you get."

"I found something called the Great Railroad Conspiracy of 1851."

"Yes! Tell me about it."

"Okay, it says here, 'Abel F. Fitch, a Connecticut native and prosperous Michigan Center landowner, headed the local opposition to the railroad. His brother-in-law ran a tavern in town that was the meeting place for the group. On April 15, 1851, in Detroit, the Michigan Central depot was destroyed by fire. Fitch was arrested with thirty-two others and charged with arson. Public opinion, fueled by one-sided newspaper reports, ran strongly against the jailed men. The judge set bail so high that none of the accused plotters could afford to get out to prepare for trial or to escape the summer heat and sickness of the detention cells.

"'The trial began May 14, 1851, and went to the jury September 25. During their internment through the hot summer months, Abel Fitch and another man died of dysentery. Public opinion turned against the railroad. A police informer who had come up with the original accusation was discredited. Eventually twelve were found guilty and the rest exonerated. Those convicted were all pardoned and released by 1855, except for one who died in prison.'"

Suddenly, the lightbulb went off in Alan's head. "Yeah, I am willing to bet that the tavern was where they held Freemason meetings. It is probably a Freemason lodge now. This Able Fitch was a thirty-third degree Freemason. He got thirty-two others each representing their degree in the order. This is the connection were seeking. So the building that they destroyed, what is it?"

"The Michigan Central Depot was burned again in 1913. They renovated it and it began to prosper again during World War II, but as more people started to drive automobiles, this is after all the Motor City, railroad use declined. After more buyouts and takeovers the, depot shut down for good on January 5, 1988. The depot has not been operational since."

"Is the building decaying, do you know?"

"Yes."

"This is the building I am seeking. Where is it?"

"It is on Fifteenth Street. Do you know how to get to Roosevelt Park?"

"Yes."

"Roosevelt Park takes you right there. It will be easier if you get on the Lodge freeway."

Just then, the receptionist approach Alan and she said, "Sir, we are closing."

Alan responded back, "The Freemasons should know that I am closing on them. Thank you, miss. Have a good night."

CHAPTER 26

As Alan arrived at the Michigan Central Depot, the scenery was just breathtaking. Detroit, which is on the western edge of the eastern time zone, during daylight savings time, can produce some beautiful sunsets at nine o'clock at night. The sky was produces some truly unique colors. The skyline had some purple, pink, and orange, all with a milky tint. Think of it like the northern lights in Technicolor. The lights coming off the Ambassador Bridge also add to the marvelous lighting effect.

The building itself was majestic. The building looked like an old, converted church standing over eighteen stories tall. The entrance looked like a Roman Bath adorned with Guastavino arches and columns. Alan, accustomed to the arts, first thought it was a Renaissance museum. The building had been secured by a fence with barbed wire at the top. The building has been prone to vandalism in the 1990s. Alan had seen where a portion of the fence had been cut. Alan, with his skinny frame, was able to squeeze right through the cut portion of the fence.

Alan walked through the entrance, which was in the form of a giant arch. As he continued to walk inside, Alan could see the stones were crumbling and deteriorating along the arches and columns. The depot looked as if it had truly been abandoned. There were holes in the walls and graffiti painted everywhere on the walls. The veneer was peeling off the walls. The building was so big; Alan had no clue where to look for Melissa. Then he noticed something in the graffiti. Someone has spray painted the symbol of Freemasonry on the wall with an arrow painted next to it. Alan followed the arrow, which led him to the room where the arcade room used to be.

The arcade room looked to be in better condition than the rest of the depot. In the arcade room Alan was staring at two large Tuscan columns with more graffiti on them. The Freemason symbol told Alan to walk through a dark hallway. The hallway was dark, but you could see light at the end of the hallway. The light at the end was very bright, mainly because the passageway was so dark, the light shined in the eyes of Alan so bright he had to narrow his eyes to keep from going blind.

Through the arcade room and down the long, dark hallway, Alan was now in the room where the ticket counter used to be. The light had returned to normal and Alan could see more freemason symbols telling him to go left. Alan turned to the left around the corner of where the counter used to be. The counter has completely fallen apart. The debris from the stand has been littered all over the ground. To the right, Alan sees an elevator, but just as expected, the elevator is inoperable. Alan decided to continue in the direction of another dark hallway. This time, Alan could hardly see any light at the end of it.

Alan just kept walking straight even though there was no light and he couldn't see a thing. As soon as Alan walked through the hallway, he had entered the concourse of the depot. Suddenly, copper lights were turned on, and Alan could see a host of people wearing tuxedoes and Freemason jewels and regalia. Two Freemasons jumped Alan from behind and pointed a gun at his back.

A man who was at Alan's back said, "Excellent, the last piece in this chess game has arrived. Thank you, Alan, for following up on that clue that we provided you." That man with his back to Alan turned around, and it was State Representative Tony Kiebler. "I regret that it has come to this point, but you are so damn clever, Alan, that you have become a problem and we need to take care of it."

What was more peculiar to Alan was the fact that the floor had been redesigned into black-and-white squares. The whole floor of the concourse had been redesigned into a large chessboard. Some of the Freemasons dressed in black tuxedoes had taken their places on the board. Alan's photographic memory was starting to come back to him. In his research he recalled photographs he has seen that shows some Masonic halls having marble black-and-white squares for their floor.

Kiebler said, "I believe you are looking for Melissa. Well, she is right over there in her proper position as the white queen."

Melissa was dressed in a white gown and handcuffed to the bars that acted as a window to the concourse. A Freemason that was diagonally from her, wearing a crown with a cross at the top, had a gun pointed at her. Alan was clearly outnumbered about thirteen to one.

"Knights," Kiebler ordered, "Mr. Williams is not in his proper position, please put him in the white king square next to the white queen and handcuff him to the bars."

Alan immediately went to talk with Melissa. "Don't worry, Melissa, Patrick and Lorenzo will be on their way."

"I am afraid not, Mr. Williams. We left them a crumb that will lead them to the Broderick Tower. They will never find you. As you can see, we are about to put you in checkmate."

"You're a murderous son of a bitch, you can never get way with all you have done!" screamed Melissa.

"Rooks, would you gag both of them. I am happy to talk, but it will be in a civil tone," said Kiebler. "How do you like what we have done with the place?"

"Oh, I love what you have done, I was thinking about purchasing this place for my new office," said Alan sarcastically, while the rooks were gagging Melissa.

"The police thought the mayor was renovating this place to be their new headquarters. No, he is renovating the depot for us," Kiebler continued on as his rooks gagged Alan and Melissa, "See, we have been pulling you by the strings. We orchestrated every move you made in the course of the investigation, except for one, which is the reason why you're here. I threw Dr. Leyland out there as a curveball to you. I knew it was a pitch you could not resist, Alan. I knew how you were so wholly against vaccines. Granted, you are right to be against them. Vaccines are part of our eugenics program."

Alan and Melissa gave back a stare like they never heard what eugenics was.

"Oh, I see. You don't know what eugenics is. Well, I would be happy to tell you. Eugenics is the study of the agencies under social control that seek to improve or impair the racial qualities of future generations, whether physically or mentally. Sir Francis Galton, an English mathematician, coined the term in 1883. Galton saw a new branch of scientific inquiry that ranks and orders human beings' worth. At the turn of the century, his ideas found an audience in the United States, but mainly those who belong in the elite class. Bohemian Grove, which is a branch of our organization, is part of that class. I will spare you the history and get into what we are doing with it today.

"The resurgence and repackaging of the same eugenics 'science' has found a new voice. 'Overpopulation,' 'carbon footprint,' 'economic burden,' 'environmentalism,' are some of the terms that if you pay attention, you will hear everywhere today. The news is full of stories about children are the biggest problem as far as the carbon footprint goes and stories about how marriage is bad and doesn't make you happy. The *Times* recently reported that it is irresponsible to have more than two children, that it creates an unbearable burden on the environment. Speaker of the House, Nancy Pelosi, stated that 'family planning services are a must during these economic times.' One of the first decisions Obama made after taking office was to reverse the ban on funding of international family planning groups that provide abortion services. Don't be deceived by these and other terms, it is eugenics."

As Kiebler was speaking, Melissa could not believe what she was hearing and thought this guy was crazy. Alan was thinking just how diabolical this criminal has been all along.

Kiebler was continuing on, "Yes, we are poisoning the food supply with high-fructose corn syrup, monosodium glutamate, that cheeseburger you ate at McDonald's has ammonium in it. Let us not forget the aspartame that is in your gum and the fluoride in your water. We bombard your advertising with psychotropic drugs that are worse than heroin and cocaine. The best part is the general public swallows it up, because they have no other alternative."

Kiebler was acting all giddy, and then suddenly he changed his demeanor to a more somber tone.

"However, let me tell you that eugenics is really about reducing the world population to a level where we, the elite class like it. We want to have the world to ourselves, and you, people, get in our way. We would like the level to drop to about five hundred billion, but we keep hitting snags. For instance, not many people are taking the vaccines as we would like. I could go on and on, because our plan is just so great, but I must get down to the business with you two.

"The plan was going along fine. You were going after Dr. Leyland, who was just a pawn in this chess game, and I as a congressman working my way up would have railed the vaccine policy and run on a global warming platform and work to get cap and trade policies, which is our new scam. It is the key that is going to let us rule the world.

"You, Alan, however, had to perform a move we weren't expecting. You had a Freemason go and infiltrate our own order. It was quite genius how you arranged with Lieutenant Patrick. Knowing that I was member in the lodge and not Dr. Leyland would have tipped you off, so that is why we are here at this moment right now."

Melissa tried to talk through her gag, but the sound was muffled, and no one could understand what she was trying to ask.

"Go ahead, rooks, let her ask her question."

"How did you kill Mark Lewis when you were in the office at the time of the murder?"

"Yes, I bribed my secretary to tell you that answer."

Alan was trying to talk too, but again no one could understand him.

"All right, let him ask his question."

"Why did you kill Lewis and Thomas and why were you trying to kill us at the airport?"

"The airport, now that was a bit of fun, wasn't it? We chased you in the airport, just to intimidate you, not to kill you. In fact my two rooks were the drivers in that episode. The reason why Lewis and Thomas died was Thomas broke the cardinal rule. Thomas told the alternative media, the ones viewed as radical and extreme, he told about our plans in the secret meetings without authorization. We preprogram the public through television and then decide when and what we are going to tell them to keep them brainwashed. It is called predictive programming. Thomas was feeding censored information to the media. He broke his oath, so we had to kill him. Lewis and Thomas were lovers. Lewis's love for Thomas outweighed his loyalty to the order, and he was threatening to tell Woolery. Luckily, I got to him before he got a chance to talk to Woolery."

Kiebler took a glance at his watch and decided he needed to get going.

"Well, I really enjoyed this little chat, but I must move on with my agenda. Bishop, you can capture the white queen now."

CHAPTER 27

The bishop cocked his revolver, which was aiming for the heart of Melissa. Just then, a roar came through in the distance out of hallway where Alan had entered from. Suddenly, men that looked like mascots of the New England Patriots with long rifles were shooting at the Freemasons. Alan and Melissa looked at each other and didn't know whether to be thankful or scared.

"What the hell," Kiebler said, exasperated.

Immediately, the Patriots, which there about thirty of them, shot the bishop, then they shot the rooks, then they shot the knights, pretty soon the chessboard was clearing itself of pieces. The Freemasons got ambushed and could not handle the onslaught they were enduring. The few Freemasons that were still alive during the shoot-out escaped on the other side of the concourse. Among them was Representative Kiebler.

A man dressed like Paul Revere walked in and said, "Do not be afraid, we mean you no harm." A couple of the Patriots took off the gag and freed Alan and Melissa.

Alan spoke first, "Who are you?"

"We are the Oath Keepers. A nonpartisan association of former military, veterans, police officers, and firefighters who *will* fulfill the oath we swore to support and defend the Constitution against all enemies, foreign and domestic, so help us God. We are guardians of the republic. Think of us like your guardian angels."

"Well, thank you, but how did you know we were here?"

"First, let me explain our mission. We Oath Keepers have a couple of axioms. One is we will not just follow orders and the other is not on our watch. Our oath is to the Constitution, not to the politicians, and we will not obey unconstitutional (and thus illegal) and immoral orders, such as orders to disarm the American people or to place them under martial law and deprive them of their ancient right to jury trial. We do not advocate the overthrow of the government and we do not advocate violence. If you, the American people, are forced to once again fight for your liberty in another American Revolution, you will not be alone. We will stand with you.

"Now, Alan, your name was floating around in our association that you might be a strong possible candidate for our association. News had broken that you were helping the police with the Mark Lewis murder, so I decided to catch you at the police station. Before I walked inside, I witnessed the congressman kidnapping your girlfriend. I followed them without them spotting me. Once I knew they were hiding here, I got a few dozen of my men, we all have experience in these matters, and proceeded to take the action as you just witnessed."

"After saving our lives, I will definitely give it some serious thought. What about Kiebler?"

"I posted a dozen men by the side entrance, they should nab him. I also called 911. The police should be here at any moment."

"You have done well, my friend."

"By the way, Samuel is the name, Samuel Adams. You take care and keep making sure the police are abiding by the constitutional oath they swore. You don't know how vital it is."

"Oh, yes, I do. Believe me, I only know full well now."

CHAPTER 28

It felt good for both Alan and Melissa to step outside in the warm night air. The skyline does not have so many milky colors, but the moonlight reflecting off the Detroit River made for a serene and tranquil setting. A parade of disco lights was parked along Fifteenth Street. Sergeant Lorenzo and Lieutenant Patrick came up walking on the street to meet up with Alan and Melissa. For the first time, all four of them were happy to see each other.

Lorenzo spoke first, "How are you guys doing?"

"We are a bit tired, exhausted, but are truly happy to be alive."

"We arrested Kiebler. He will be looking at two counts of murder, four counts of attempted murder, and kidnapping."

"I hope they kill him," said Melissa.

"I doubt that, because Michigan doesn't have the death penalty, but he should get life without parole," said Alan.

"I don't know, Kiebler is going to get a high-priced legal representation, he may plea-bargain and only get ten to twenty, said Lorenzo.

Patrick chimed in and said, "You know what gets me more than anything else in this case?"

"What is it, sir?" questioned Lorenzo.

"The mayor actually thinking that this dump was going to be our new headquarters. He was certainly one crazy fool."

Lorenzo, Alan, and Melissa all laughed at Patrick.

Lorenzo then said, "You know, Alan. If you had died in that depot, I would have missed you. I am starting to get fond of you."

"Back off, miss, that is my man," said Melissa in a firm voice.

"Easy, Melissa, I don't mean like that. No, I meant as in an investigative capacity. What do you say, Lieutenant? Is Alan ready to be on the force?"

"Maybe, I will tell you what I will do. I will go to the board and ask for a review."

"Well, I am just getting all kinds of job offers when I could find nothing a week ago!"

Patrick spoke up, "After seeing you in action for one case, I can safely say, you are one hell of a detective. If the board approves your review, I would be honored to command you."

Alan and Melissa had some unfinished business back at the station. They needed to give their statement to the police, which would be used as evidence in the upcoming trial. Alan and Melissa were walking in the hallway when he saw the police escort Tony Kiebler, in handcuffs, to the lockup. Alan turned to the hallway that ran parallel to where Kiebler was walking. Alan tapped on the window to get Kiebler's attention. Kiebler stopped and turned to look at Alan. Alan said one word and one word only that got into the nerve of Kiebler, "Checkmate." After that, Alan walked away from Kiebler.

Melissa drove Alan back to their home office back in Jackson. The two of them could not have been happier to be home safe and sound.

"What music should we listen to for the night?" asked Melissa.

"Let us celebrate with some Tchaikovsky just like at the end of *V for Vendetta*."

"Well, Alan, I hope we have another adventure like the one we just had. That was fun and exciting."

"Fun and exciting? We almost got killed!"

"Yeah, I know, but we came out of it alive, we won, and we beat the master criminal. Those two elements make it fun and exciting for me."

"I don't know which makes me luckier, dozens of guardian angels dressed like Boston Tea Partiers protecting me or you for a girlfriend."

"Why don't you come to bed with me tonight and find out the answer?"